MURDER AT LOWRY HOUSE

HAZEL MARTIN MYSTERIES BOOK 1

LEIGHANN DOBBS

CHAPTER ONE

"**R**eally, Alice, don't you think the tang of arsenic would be detectable in a scone?" Hazel Martin cocked her head and watched her long-time cook, Alice Duprey, vigorously beat the mixture in a yellow stoneware bowl.

Alice scrunched her face. "Well, now that you mention it, madam, it does have a bitter aftertaste, don' it?"

"Technically, the arsenic itself is neutral, but it can change the flavor of the food. Most people say it creates a metallic taste." Hazel rifled through one of the two notebooks which lay open on the scuffed pine table in front of her.

As a novelist, Hazel kept copious notes on various methods of murder, and poisoning was her favorite. She found the page on arsenic and verified her statement then tapped her green celluloid fountain pen on the other notebook while she thought.

A misshapen blob of ink splattered onto the middle of the empty page, as if to taunt her that she had yet to come up with a satisfactory opening scene for her next murder mystery. "Perhaps we could put the arsenic in something else instead. Marmalade has a strong natural taste. That might hide it."

"Indeed." Alice looked thoughtful as she turned the dough onto the floured stainless steel counter and kneaded it slightly.

Hazel knew that most ladies of the manor didn't hang around in the kitchen consulting the help on matters of murder, but the kitchen at Hastings Manor had been one of her favorite places since childhood. She took comfort in the familiarity of the meticulously scrubbed black-and-white tile, the golden glow of the finely polished oak cabinets, and the copper jelly molds that glinted in the sunlight streaming down from windows set high on the wall.

Even the stacks of yellow-glazed pottery mixing bowls that lined the pine shelves on the large hutch that dominated one wall reminded her of carefree childhood days when she would have naught to do but hang around the gardens and kitchen, hoping Cook would let her lick the mixing bowl.

But Hazel was no longer a child, nor was she carefree. She was a widow. A grown woman with a book to write and precious few ideas on how to start it.

Alice looked at Hazel out of the corner of her eye. "Detective Chief Inspector Gibson would know the best way to use arsenic."

Hazel looked down at her notebook, not wanting Alice to see the pang of sadness that stabbed through her. Alice's mentioning of the inspector had become more and more frequent, and while she knew the cook only had her best interests at heart, Hazel's late husband, Charles, had only been dead three years. Just the thought of anyone else being interested in her —which Gibson clearly was—made her anxious with guilt. It was much too soon for Hazel to think about someone else, even if Inspector Gibson did have kind eyes.

An inspector with Scotland Yard, Charles had been killed while chasing down a dangerous suspect, and the empty hole he'd left behind was like a raw wound that wouldn't heal. The pain had lessened slightly over the past three years, but it was still there front and center as a reminder of what Hazel would never have again.

Hazel missed him terribly and not only because

they had truly been in love, but also because he'd been invaluable for the consultations in various methods of murder that he often supplied for her mystery novels.

And now, here she was, trying to write the first one after his death and coming up mostly empty. What if she couldn't write one on her own without his guidance? Did Alice think she couldn't, and was that why she kept mentioning Gibson?

No, of course not. Alice had all the faith in the world in her, as did her entire staff. And they were depending on her, as were her publisher and millions of readers, so she'd better get cracking.

Hazel absently wiped at the ink splotches that seemed to permanently stain her fingers. The ink stains reminded her that she needed to get some words on paper soon, or her publisher was going to start to nag at her. Her current mystery involved a poisoning during breakfast, and she was trying to decide between arsenic, strychnine, or hemlock. "Maybe hemlock would be better. It tastes like carrots. We could disguise it in a root dish. Of course, then I might have to change the venue from breakfast to dinner," she muttered, mostly to herself.

"*Mew.*"

Alice whipped her head around at the sound. In

the doorway sat a sleek Siamese cat. His intelligent pale-blue eyes were striking in contrast to the dark-brown mask that covered most of his face. His body was a creamy mocha color, and his legs, tail, and ears matched the mink-brown color of his face. His gaze darted from the broom in the corner to Alice. The cat, whose name was Dickens, was Hazel's constant companion and somewhat of a sleuth in his own right. He also delighted in tormenting Alice, who felt that cats did not belong in the house, much less in the kitchen.

"Oh, no you don't!" Alice lunged for the broom, and Dickens hissed at her. "Not in my kitchen, you overgrown rat." Alice swatted the broom in the air like a swashbuckler wielding a sword. Dickens ran around the kitchen, weaving and dodging around the swooshing broom, apparently finding the game fun.

"If you weren't so good at catching mice around here, I'd have you banished!" Alice yelled.

"*Meow!*" Dickens gave a haughty cry as if to tell Alice that Hazel would allow no such thing and then scampered out of the kitchen. Alice, her face beet red with the effort, put the broom back with an exasperated sigh and smoothed her apron before returning to her task of shaping the dough into round scones.

"I don't know why you like that creature so

much." Alice opened one of the large ovens, letting out wisps of steam and the sweet aroma of fresh-baked scones.

Hazel laughed. She knew Alice would never do anything to harm the cat. In fact, she suspected Alice secretly liked Dickens, and had even once caught her slipping a morsel of fish to the feisty feline.

"Come on, Alice, you know that Dickens is my confidant," Hazel said. "He knows all my secrets and has helped solve a few mysteries of his own."

"Speaking of which…" Maggie, Hazel's house-maid, appeared in the doorway. "I hope you haven't forgotten about that strange invitation."

Hazel's hand flew to her pocket, the crisp paper crinkling as her fingers brushed against it. She took it out, a frown creasing her face as she glanced down at it. "Yes, that's right. This is rather disturbing, isn't it?"

The lavender-colored paper had become wrinkled in the pocket of her dress. She placed it flat on the table and smoothed it out. It was a pretty paper —heavy quality stock, lavender in color, with a cluster of vibrant lilacs stamped in the top right corner. A subtle, flowery aroma wafted up as she looked down at the spidery writing, which looked to have come from a Parker dip pen with a wide nib. An early model, if her guess was correct. And

Hazel's guesses about pens were almost always correct. She was somewhat of an expert on the topic.

DEAR HAZEL,

I IMPLORE you to attend the weekend celebration of my eightieth birthday starting this Friday, 25th July, at Lowry House. I need your help, as I fear one of my relatives wants this birthday to be my last. Please tell no one you received this letter and make it appear as if you simply stopped by to bring your birthday wishes on a whim.

SINCERELY,

MYRTLE PEMBROKE

MAGGIE HAD COME to stand beside her, wisps of brown hair sticking out from her cap, her face eager with excitement. Mysteries were not only Hazel's vocation in writing, but somewhat of a hobby for her and her entire household staff. "Indeed, it does seem mysterious."

"But Myrtle is quite old. Why would someone want to do her in?" Alice asked as she slid a tray containing large round pieces of dough into the oven.

Hazel tapped her lips with her index finger. "Myrtle is wealthy, but it hardly seems wise to kill her when she is already eighty years old."

"True, but something must be going on, or she wouldn't have written, and you haven't had a mystery to solve in quite some time. This could be just the thing you need," Maggie said.

"And you know looking into other mysteries always helps with the writin' of yer books." Alice nodded toward the empty notebook where Hazel had scribbled out several scenarios. She *was* a bit stuck on her plot, and Myrtle was a dear old friend of her parents. It would be terribly rude of her to ignore the woman's request.

Alice slid a plate of scones onto the table in front of Hazel, who eyed them dubiously considering their recent conversation.

Alice raised a brow. "Scone, madam?"

Hazel's eyes flicked from the scones to Alice and then Maggie. She could see by the anxious looks on their faces that the two women were just as eager for her to get "unstuck" with her writing as she was. These women cared about her. They were more than staff. They were her family, and the success of this book—the first one since Charles's death—meant a lot to all of them. And if a little change of scenery and a mystery to solve helped get her unstuck, then she was all for it.

Hazel pushed away from the table. "Thanks, Alice, but I don't think so. I have packing to do. I'll leave first thing tomorrow for Lowry House, and if Myrtle is right about someone trying to kill her, you can bet I will get to the bottom of it."

CHAPTER TWO

The next day, it took Hazel nearly the entire morning to finish packing for both herself and Dickens, as well as field Maggie's persistent suggestions that she take her along. She could hardly bring a maid and still pretend that she was just popping by for a quick visit.

Myrtle had instructed her not tell anyone about the letter, so she planned to act as if she had been holidaying at Dunelawn By-The-Sea and had stopped by Myrtle's on the way home, since Lowry House was halfway between Hastings Manor and the famous hotel.

It was midafternoon by the time Hazel stood at the imposing oak door of Lowry House with Dickens's red-and-black hound's-tooth carrier clutched in one hand, the other grasping the cool, smooth brass of the lion's-head door knocker.

A black-suited butler answered the door, but before she could announce who she was, Myrtle swept into the polished mahogany hall, her eyes lighting on Hazel in surprised recognition.

"Lordy, if it isn't Hazel Martin!" Myrtle rushed over as if she hadn't been expecting Hazel at all, and Hazel smiled and nodded. Myrtle was putting on a good act. A pretty, young, green-eyed woman with copper hair, dressed in a slate-blue chiffon chemise— the style that was so popular with young people and that made Hazel feel positively matronly in her dowdy, navy-blue traveling outfit—appeared beside Myrtle. Hazel recognized her as Myrtle's grandniece.

"You don't look a day over seventy, Myrtle. Are you sure you don't have your birth year wrong?" Hazel teased.

The truth was, Myrtle looked and acted much younger than her eighty years. Perhaps Hazel should try to discover her secret. The old woman was positively glowing and wore a chiffon dress similar to that of her grandniece, but with a few more ruffles to hide her more mature figure. Beaded necklaces of several layers sparkled in the light from the overhead crystal chandelier. Her red hair was cut in a curly bob. Both the style and the color—which Hazel assumed came from using henna, a natural hair dye made popular by Clara Bow—would have looked ridiculous on another woman of that age, but somehow looked just right on Myrtle.

Myrtle smiled at Hazel's compliment, her hand self-consciously fluffing her hair. A cameo ring boasting a deeply carved scene of angels and cherubs framed by tiny rubies—a family heirloom that Myrtle had once told Hazel was extremely valuable—looked gigantic on Myrtle's slim finger. "Do you like my hair? Gloria gave me a little makeover. She tries to keep me young with these newfangled outfits and health elixirs." Myrtle turned to the younger woman. "Gloria, you remember my friend, Hazel Martin?"

"Of course I do. Nice to see you again." Hazel thought she detected a flash of a knowing look in the other woman's green eyes. Perhaps Myrtle had confided in Gloria about her suspicions. The two of them were very close since Gloria was her grand-niece, the granddaughter of Myrtle's now deceased sister… or perhaps Gloria was the one she was suspicious *of*.

"Where are my manners?" Myrtle clamped on to Hazel's elbow and steered her toward the drawing room, her heels clicking on the black-and-white marble floor as they crossed the hall. "Do come in and say hello to everyone."

The drawing room was steeped in rich colors: burgundy curtains, cobalt-blue, ruby, and gold Oriental carpet, and mahogany-paneled walls. The furniture consisted of highly carved walnut frames and sumptuous velvet cushions. Gold-framed oil paintings decorated the walls.

A marble fireplace adorned with carved angels dominated one end of the room. A tall, lanky man in his midfifties leaned one elbow against it, admiring a painting that hung on the wall. Across from him, a much younger man with a large bandage on his right hand snoozed in a chair. Next to that, a woman in her early to midtwenties with red hair and scarlet lips lounged on a divan, inspecting her ruby-red nails.

"Everyone, this is my friend, the novelist, Hazel Martin," Myrtle said proudly as she propelled her into the room.

"*Meow*." Dickens, not one to be left out, chose that moment to let his presence be known.

"Oh, and her cat, Dickens," Myrtle added.

The man turned from the fireplace, one brow quirked as his eyes fell on the carrier. Hazel glanced down to see that Dickens had his face pressed to the screen in the front, his intelligent eyes keenly surveying the room. She adjusted her position so the carrier was behind her.

No telling what kind of shenanigans Dickens might get up to later on if he were allowed to take inventory of the entire room from within his carrier. Truth be told, she should have left him in the car, which idled in the driveway, but the last time she'd done that, he'd coughed hairballs up on her pillow for the following two weeks. It wasn't common practice to bring one's cat in on a visit, but as a novelist, Hazel was expected to be a bit eccentric, and since she was somewhat of a celebrity, people didn't seem to mind when she brought Dickens along. Some had even come to expect it.

Undaunted, Myrtle continued with the introductions. "Hazel, this is my son, Edward…you've probably met before…my grandson, Wes, and his wife, Vera."

Hazel's family had been close with Myrtle's family at one time, so of course she'd met Edward many times before. And she knew Wes was the son of Myrtle's deceased daughter, Sarah.

Thinking about Myrtle losing Sarah reminded Hazel of her loss of Charles, and she was overwhelmed with a rush of compassion and a feeling of camaraderie for the older woman. Hazel was now even more determined to get to the bottom of Myrtle's suspicions, be they real or not.

Hazel nodded at Edward, Wes's sleeping form, and Vera.

Edward said pleasantly, "Nice to see you again, Mrs. Martin."

Vera stood, her lavishly beaded deep-blue dress sparkling in the light, and large diamonds winking in her ears. "Nice to meet you."

Wes shifted position in the chair and let out a snore.

Vera approached the cat carrier and bent down to peer inside. "Don't mind my husband. He spends most of his days asleep." She slid a fingernail through the mesh in the front and scratched Dickens. "What a darling creature. I should get a picture."

She picked a square leather box up off the table that Hazel recognized as a box camera similar to the Brownie camera that was all the rage in the States. She'd used the same model often to capture images of scenes she wanted to depict in her novels, and Charles had used much more complex models in his police work.

Vera stood back from the carrier and held the camera at her waist, looking down to take the shot.

Dickens hissed and promptly presented her with his backside, to the laughter of Myrtle and Edward.

"Looks like he doesn't want his picture taken," Edward said.

Vera shrugged. "Maybe next time. We could do with a cat at the cottage… get rid of the rats."

"Rats?" Myrtle seemed shocked.

Vera straightened. "Yes, I told you I have to keep all the food in the pantry for fear they'll eat it."

"There are no rats. You're lucky Mother is nice enough to let you live there," Edward cut in.

"Yes, you are lucky. The rest of us have to fend for ourselves." Hazel turned to see a dour-looking young woman standing in the doorway. She had mousey-brown hair, and though she looked to be around the same age as Gloria and Vera, her clothing looked more suitable for a woman twenty years her senior. Her lips were turned down as if in disapproval as her dark eyes scanned the room, coming to rest on Dickens's carrier, which by now was starting to get rather heavy in Hazel's hand.

"*Merow.*" Dickens's voice was loud, and Hazel figured he was probably trying to signal that he was tired of being cooped up.

"Oh, Hazel, this my granddaughter, Fran.

Edward's daughter." Myrtle gestured between Hazel and Fran. "Hazel is a dear friend of the family."

Fran looked at her and squinted. "Yes, I remember. The novelist, I believe?"

Hazel nodded. She readied herself to fend off a potential fan, as happened all too often, but instead, Fran pressed her lips together then crossed to a chair on the opposite side of the room and sank into its lush, velvet-tufted cushions.

Hazel sensed tension in the air. No wonder Myrtle thought someone was up to no good. The family didn't seem overly friendly toward each other.

She shifted the cat carrier to her other hand. "Well, you certainly have a houseful, Myrtle."

"Yes, indeed. Everyone is staying for my birthday celebration. Oh, you simply must stay, too!" Myrtle clapped her hands together and turned wide eyes to Hazel, as if she'd just thought of Hazel staying.

"Well, I don't know…" Hazel looked around uncertainly so as to add credence to Myrtle's act.

"Oh, but you must," Myrtle insisted. "We have a whole weekend of activities planned. It will be great fun. And how many times do I get to turn eighty?"

"That sounds lovely," Hazel said. "I do have my bags from holiday in the car, but I wouldn't want to put you to any trouble…"

"It will be no trouble at all," Gloria cut in. "I'll go see if Mrs. Naughton can make you up a room, and I'll have your driver bring your bags up."

Edward scowled. "Mother, I hardly see how Hazel would want to be included in our little family celebration. I'm sure she has better places to be."

"Nonsense. Hazel is an old friend. I'm sure she'd love to spend the weekend with us." Myrtle turned and winked at Hazel. "We have a nice tea planned and outdoor games. Walks in the garden and even a formal party with a small band and champagne tomorrow night."

"Not tomorrow, dear," Vera said. "The party is Saturday. Tomorrow is Friday."

A look of confusion contorted Myrtle's face, then it cleared. "Why, of course it is. That's exactly what I meant. Saturday."

"Well, if Hazel *wants* to stay, then she is certainly welcome." Edward picked up a Staffordshire figure off the mantel and turned it over in his hands, looked at the bottom, then shook his head and replaced it. "Exquisite work always amazes me."

"If you recall, Edward is an antiques dealer. Always picking things up and looking underneath. Rather annoying, if you ask me," Myrtle whispered.

"I heard that," Edward said.

"Daddy just has good taste, even if he is a bit materialistic," Fran said softly, her fingers fiddling with a deeply carved cameo at her throat which bore a resemblance to the ring on Myrtle's finger. Hazel was just about to ask about it when a servant appeared at the door.

"Mrs. Martin's room is ready."

"Wonderful. That was very fast, Mrs. Naughton." Myrtle turned to Hazel. "I'm sure you want to freshen up. Mrs. Naughton will show you the way."

Hazel nodded to the others in the room and followed Mrs. Naughton toward the wide, sweeping staircase, pausing just below the first stair to chance a look back into the drawing room.

Clearly the family was at odds, but that wasn't entirely unusual. Most families had some sort of tension from time to time. But if Myrtle was right about *this* family, there was more than just tension in the air…there was also murder.

CHAPTER THREE

I t was with much relief that Hazel set the cat carrier on the floor and shook the circulation back into her fingers as she surveyed the lavishly appointed room.

Done in tones of lavender and gray, the room boasted lush velvet curtains, a sumptuous silk Oriental rug in tones of light purple, green, and gold, matching silk bedding, a dainty plum-colored velvet settee with rose-carved walnut frame, and most importantly, a large, ornately carved desk under a window overlooking the garden. A small marble fireplace adorned one wall. In front of it were two overstuffed armchairs in plum velvet.

"Oh, this is just lovely," Hazel said out loud even though she was alone.

"*Merooooo!*" Dickens yelled, reminding her he was still trapped in the carrier.

Hazel bent down and opened the front door of the carrier. Dickens shot out in an angry blur of cream-colored fur, stopping a good eight feet from the carrier to shake his paws and look disdainfully back at it over his shoulder before peering up at Hazel reproachfully.

"Sorry, didn't mean to keep you cooped up in there." Hazel set about unpacking her leather suitcases, including all of Dickens's paraphernalia, which she set up first so he would have all the comforts of home.

"*Merow.*" Dickens's tone was less accusatory this time. He gave an approving sniff of his royal-blue silk cat bed, which Hazel had placed in front of the fireplace, and then skulked around the perimeter of the room, exploring every corner as Hazel finished putting her clothes in the gilt-and-maple veneer armoire then changed into a more formal burgundy-colored dress with just a hint of beading on the bodice for dinner.

Hazel hadn't yet been quite brave enough to adopt the thin sheath dresses that younger women wore even though, at the age of thirty-nine, she still had the figure for them. She still liked to keep with the times, but favored a bit of a more sophisticated look.

As a married woman, she'd never worried much about fashion. Her thoughts were all about her books and her characters. Maybe now she should reconsider her wardrobe. Though the younger fashions might look silly on her with the strands of gray that were starting to sneak into her hair. Maybe she should find out where Myrtle and Vera got their henna.

As was her routine, she saved the best of her unpacking chores for last. She lifted a finely tooled leather case out of her suitcase and opened it carefully. Inside was her collection of fountain pens. A dubonnet-red Esterbrook, a jade radite Sheaffer, her old standby celluloid green Parker duofold pen, and the Waterman sterling silver filigree pen given to her by Charles upon publication of her first novel twelve years ago.

She lifted the Waterman out of its slot and traced her fingers over the chased filigree design, allowing herself to indulge in a feeling of sadness and loss. But only for a moment, as Hazel didn't like to dwell on the past. Even without Charles, she had a bright future and a good life. She quickly released the pen, placing it on the desk, and then took the other pens out and lined them up in a row.

The center of the desk had thoughtfully been fitted with a stack of notepaper, the same lavender paper that had been used to write the note Hazel had received from Myrtle, summoning her to Lowry House. She wondered if Myrtle had piles of it in every guest room as well as on her own personal writing desk. She set the paper aside, taking out her notebook and laying it open on the center of the desk. She had a few hours before dinner and was hoping to get a few words written for her current book.

She picked up the Waterman, uncapped it, and gazed out the window. "I do suppose I could use hemlock and put it in a carrot jelly. That way I could still keep the breakfast scenario."

"*Mew.*" Dickens hopped up onto the edge of her desk, looking at her with intelligent opalescent-blue eyes. He sat, curling his mink-colored tail around his front paws gracefully.

"I'm glad you agree. Though I'll have to ask Alice how, exactly, one would make a carrot jelly that would be sweet enough for breakfast. Too bad I've sent Duffy home with the car already. I could have instructed him to ask her and return with a recipe." For the next twenty minutes, Hazel scribbled in the notebook, and the page became filled with dark-blue

words and unsightly blobs of ink where she paused
the pen in thought. Her fingers became dotted with
new ink stains, but she didn't notice, as she was too
caught up in the story and crafting the words to
convey the murderous breakfast scenario.

Apparently realizing he was being ignored,
Dickens jumped down from the desk and embarked
on another, more detailed exploration of the room.
He darted under the bed and peered out from the
bed skirt. Then he batted at the gold piping on the
edge of the skirt, causing it to sway back and forth
while he tried to play catch with it. Finally, he rolled
out from under the bed, leapt sideways, and scurried
under one of the chairs.

Hazel turned away from his antics and was
vaguely aware of him leaping up onto a bookcase,
running across the top of the mantel, and then situ-
ating himself in the fireplace, where he sniffed
profusely before trotting over to the bureau and shim-
mying underneath.

"*Merooow!*" Dickens howled from the bureau as if
he'd discovered something immensely important, and
seconds later, the pink pads of his paw appeared from
underneath the edge as he batted a small yellow
object across the room.

The object skittered across the floorboards barely

an inch from the edge of the rug and stopped next to Hazel's chair.

"What's this?" She bent down and picked it up. It was a sprig of buttercups twined together as if to make a bouquet. "I wonder where these came from."

"*Mewp.*" Dickens shimmied out from under the bureau and shook himself off, looking at her with a bored expression as if to say, "That's for you to discover. I did the hard part of finding it."

"Hmmm." Hazel glanced around the room, her eyes stopping at a small vase on the table beside the bed. It was filled with lilacs. Hazel wondered where they'd gotten them, as it was past season. Maybe there was a florist that supplied them from some exotic place? The upstairs maid had probably set fresh flowers out when she'd made up the room. She twirled the yellow flowers in her hand. These were brown. Perhaps they had been in a vase for a previous guest.

She looked around for a wastepaper basket. Finding a lovely receptacle of weaved willow, she tossed them in. The colors of the trash bin reminded her of something else—the cameo that Myrtle's granddaughter, Fran, had been wearing.

Hazel hadn't had a chance to ask, but she was almost certain it matched Myrtle's ring, and she was also almost certain Fran had some sort of issue or problem with the cameo. It was the possessive manner in which Fran had been touching it.

If the cameos had been passed down from generations, did Fran have some sort of grudge over them?

Was that grudge strong enough for her to consider murder?

Hazel didn't have time to think about it because just then a knock sounded at her door, and Mrs. Naughton called out, "Dinner!"

Hazel capped her pen, flipped her notebook closed, and stood. Then she smoothed the silk skirts of her dress and followed Mrs. Naughton down to dinner.

CHAPTER FOUR

The dining room at Lowry House was steeped in elegance. The table was set with fine china and sterling silver cutlery. Sparkling Waterford crystal goblets reflected prisms of light from the two chandeliers above the table. The room was filled with family antiques. A massive hunt board complete with high-relief carvings of foxes and antlered stags in dark mahogany dominated one end of the room. The table itself could seat more than twenty people, though only seven places had been set.

Though the room was dominated by Myrtle's ancestors' antiques, including some of the ancestors themselves, who peered down from gilt-framed oil paintings, it also included some modern touches. In the middle of the hunt board, a green onyx geometric-shaped clock ticked away the minutes.

Spaced along the perimeter of the walls, shell-shaped alabaster sconces nestled within pierced brass brackets cast beams of light toward the ceiling, and a cathedral-topped radio sat silent on one of the side tables.

Myrtle sat at the head of the table, with Edward on her right. She indicated for Hazel to sit on her left. Myrtle, Vera, and Gloria had changed into more formal wear, and now their dresses were more heavily beaded and their jewelry more abundant. Only Fran remained in her dowdy outfit from earlier that afternoon.

The dinner of lamb, potatoes, and asparagus was divine. Probably one of the tastiest Hazel had had in a long time, and would've rivaled any good restaurant. Hazel would have to take care not to compliment the cooking too much, though, when she got home. Alice always asked about the meals and was very sensitive about her cooking.

"Did you find your room sufficient?" Myrtle asked Hazel.

"Yes. It's beautiful. The little touches are so thoughtful. Especially the lilac writing paper. Do you provide paper for all your guests?"

Myrtle smiled. "Yes, providing the notepaper is something my mother started a long time ago. She always said people liked to write letters in the rooms. She had special papers made for each room because each room has a theme. Yours is the lilac room. I use a gardenia pattern myself … or is it Lily of the Valley?"

Gloria rested her hand on Myrtle's arm. "It's gardenia."

Myrtle nodded. "Right. Of course. The lilac was always a favorite. I didn't realize we had much of that left. I'm glad you thought to put it in the room, Gloria."

Gloria blinked. "What?"

"Hazel's room. Didn't you set it up with Mrs. Naughton?"

Gloria glanced around the table then lowered her voice. "No, Auntie. I haven't even been in that wing in ages."

Hazel couldn't miss the look of concern on Gloria's face. Was Myrtle's assertion that Gloria had made up the room a worrisome sign of a faulty memory or just a normal assumption?

"Oh, I could have sworn." Myrtle shrugged. "Well, anyway, my mother always said a woman's notepaper was like a calling card, which is why I always use the same style. Of course, I don't write much anymore." Myrtle held up her hand, showing knuckles slightly bent. "I have a touch of arthritis."

Hazel remembered the spidery writing on the note she'd received and realized her handwriting was one of the few things that gave away her age. But the handwriting wasn't the only thing: it seemed as if Myrtle's memory might not be what it used to be, either. Apparently, no matter how much you tried to stave off aging, it had its ways of catching up. Still, it was clear that Myrtle had many more years left.

Except that, according to Myrtle, someone—possibly someone seated at this very table—wanted to cut those years short.

Her narrowed eyes scanned the table. Hard to believe she might be dining with a murderer. *Attempted* murderer, she reminded herself. And Hazel was determined to do everything in her power to make sure the next attempts, if there were any, did not become successful.

Across the table, Wes chased a piece of meat with his fork. Three misses until he finally skewered it and brought it to his lips. He was already on his fourth glass of wine. His eyes were glassy, and the few words he'd spoken slightly slurred. Vera had shot her share of nasty looks in his direction.

"The place settings here are lovely. Were they

your mother's?" Hazel had almost been afraid to touch the plates with their wide gold fleur-de-lis-patterned rims. She'd gingerly cut the meat, not wanting to use too much force for fear her knife would scratch the beautiful hand-painted scenes that decorated the face of the plate.

"Yes, they were," Myrtle said. "They're quite valuable."

"Practically priceless," Edward cut in. "I don't know why you're using them when you had me purchase the Royal Doulton settings. These plates should be in a china cabinet and not subjected to the coarse handling of foods and metal utensils."

"Or in a museum," Fran muttered, her eyes trained on her plate.

Myrtle looked down at the plates then up at Edward. "Oh, yes. the Royal Doulton. Well, since it is my eightieth birthday, I felt we should do something special and use these and not those"—Myrtle waved her hands dismissively toward the kitchen —"everyday plates."

"That's right." Gloria pinned Edward with a glare. "She wasn't going to use these, but I insisted."

"Yes, that's right. I was going to use the Royal Doulton," Myrtle said. "The willow pattern dishes."

"*Indian Tree*," Edward corrected.

"Indian Tree, like I said," Myrtle said.

Across the table, Vera hissed, and Hazel looked over to see a red stain spreading on the crisp white linen tablecloth in front of Wes. Apparently, he'd spilled his wine.

He narrowed his eyes at Vera. "You try eating with a broken hand. I'm right handed, you know. Sch'not easy," Wes slurred.

"I imagine that must be rather difficult." Hazel thought the reason for the spill had more to do with the many glasses of wine he'd had than not being able to use his right hand, but she felt it better to try to smooth the awkward situation. "How did you damage it?"

"He fell down drunk," Vera said.

"Vera!" Myrtle exclaimed. "Poor Wes has had a hard time since his mother died."

That shut everyone up, and they all focused on their plates, seemingly in a hurry to finish the meal. That was just fine with Hazel. The sooner the meal was over, the sooner she could maneuver Myrtle into a room alone and find out the details of the suspicious attempts on her life.

CHAPTER FIVE

After dinner, Hazel managed to pull Myrtle into the library. Libraries were among Hazel's most favorite rooms, and this one was extraordinary. Steeped in soft leather and the vanilla-spiced smell of old books, the room was two stories tall and lined with books, from floor to ceiling. The upper level was ringed with a balcony accessible by a spiral staircase.

Though it was July, the air cooled down after nightfall, and a pleasant breeze billowed in through the sheer curtains covering the open French doors. Hazel hesitated at the sight of so many beautiful books. Resisting the urge to rush to the bookshelves and run her fingertips along the leathery spines then carefully pull out a book and absorb herself in its pages, she settled into a buttery-soft leather armchair across from Myrtle.

Myrtle handed her a brandy, and Hazel's throat burned as she took a small sip. She wasn't much of a drinker, but she knew Myrtle was too polite to drink without her, and figured a brandy would soothe the other woman's nerves... especially given the topic they were about to discuss.

"It's so lovely to see you, Hazel. I'm glad you stopped by," Myrtle said.

"Well, I could hardly not come." Hazel decided to get down to business before they were interrupted. "Tell me about your suspicions."

Myrtle lifted a brow. "Suspicions?"

"The ones that make you think someone might be out to get you, as you wrote to me in your letter."

Myrtle's eyes clouded, and she looked down at the deep-red, blue, and gold Oriental rug. "Oh, right. *Those* suspicions. Well, I hope you won't think I'm just a silly old lady. Things have happened, but they could just be coincidence."

Hazel's eyes narrowed. Was Myrtle having second thoughts about someone trying to kill her? She sounded so uncertain now, but one didn't usually write letters summoning mystery writers to their homes to try to figure out which one of their relatives was trying to kill them if they weren't absolutely sure. Then again, Myrtle had been showing signs of forgetfulness, so maybe she didn't trust her instincts anymore.

Hazel leaned forward and touched Myrtle's knee. "Tell me what has been happening. If they are really coincidences, that will be good, won't it? Because otherwise…"

"Right. Of course." Myrtle pressed her lips together and looked up at the ceiling. "It all started about a month ago. There was an incident on my walk. I walk a regular route in the garden that skirts the steep hill on the west side of the estate. It has lovely views, and Daddy had bricks laid on the path decades ago. Part of it must've washed out under the bricks, and I had a terrible fall." Myrtle chuckled. "Gloria was with me, and you should've seen the look on her face. I took a good tumble, but she caught me, and I bounced right back up. It takes much more than a fall to do this old lady in."

Hazel tried to envision the path Myrtle was talking about. It sounded like something that could easily happen because of natural causes, but also a clever killer could have tampered with it, knowing that Myrtle walked on it every day. An old lady like Myrtle could be killed in a fall like that if she hit her head. "Washed out? You mean by rain or something?"

Myrtle nodded. "Yes. At least, that's what Wes said."

"Wes was there, too?"

"Not when I fell. Later on, I showed it to him to see what he thought about repairing it. Dooley, the gardener, shored it up with dirt and put the bricks back good as new. Though he was none too happy; seems the ground is riddled with roots, and it was a difficult job. He said it would have been hard work to dig it out enough to cause the path to be unstable on purpose." Myrtle shrugged.

The path incident might have been just due to natural causes, but Hazel was suspicious, especially since Myrtle had implied that more had happened. "But that's not the only suspicious thing that has happened, is it?"

Myrtle blanched. "Well, maybe some of the other things were my own fault."

"What do you mean?"

"I had an incident with my pills…"

"Your pills?"

"Yes, I may look young, but the truth is this old body does have some issues that need addressing. Oh, it's nothing that's going to kill me, unless, of course, I mix up my prescriptions. And that's exactly what happened." Myrtle leaned forward, obviously upset.

"But I'm so careful about those pills because I know I have to be careful, as taking too many of those heart pills can be deadly. I can't imagine I mixed things up. Some of my heart pills got in with my aspirin, and I took too many. But luckily it wasn't enough to do me in."

"Who else has access to your pills?" Hazel wondered if someone could have tampered with them. It would have been an easy way to do away with someone and make it look like an accident. But with Myrtle's memory issues, it wasn't out of the question that she might have muddled them up herself.

"I keep them in the bathroom in my suite, so anyone who was in the house could have accessed them."

"And who was in the house that day? Do you remember?"

Myrtle pressed her lips together. "It was a Tuesday. The second Tuesday in July. I remember distinctly because Mrs. Naughton noticed I was acting strangely. She called Dr. Wilkins, and he came over straightaway, because his club is only a few miles from here, and he goes there the second and fourth Tuesdays of every month. We have family dinners on Sunday, but on Tuesday no one is here. Though Fran did come right away—almost got here before the doctor."

"Your family doesn't live in?"

"No. Well, Wes and Vera are in the cottage, but they only pop in to visit me sometimes. Not that day, I don't think. Fran has a flat in town, and Charles has his own country house. He doesn't visit me so much. Of course, on special occasions like this, everyone stays at the house, but that wasn't the case that day. Gloria comes most often, but she wasn't there as she'd been away on holiday. She was very upset when she returned to find out I hadn't got in touch with her. But I would never have ruined her holiday for something silly like that. She doesn't have much money and hardly ever gets to go anywhere."

Myrtle's words piqued Hazel's interest. Money was usually the prime motivation for killing someone. She made a mental note to ask Hazel about the beneficiaries of her will.

"And then there's the indigestion," Myrtle continued.

Hazel turned her attention back on Myrtle. "Indigestion?"

Myrtle waved her hand in the air. "Honestly, I don't think it's unusual for a lady of my age to have indigestion, but I have been feeling rather sick, and I wouldn't have thought anything of it, except Gloria said—"

A soft tap on the door interrupted Myrtle. The door opened a crack, and Hazel twisted in her chair to see Gloria look in. "Oh good, you two are in here."

"Do come in, Gloria." Myrtle gestured for her to join them.

Gloria slipped into the room, closed the door softly, and took the chair beside Myrtle. It was obvious she was conflicted about something. She then leaned toward Myrtle and lowered her voice. "Did you tell her about the incidents?"

"Yes, but I don't really think—"

Gloria turned to Hazel. "Those were no accidents. Don't you agree?"

"Well, I don't know. It does seem suspicious that so many things have happened, but they all could have logical explanations."

Gloria leaned back in her chair, glancing at Myrtle. "I don't think we should take any chances. Auntie could be in danger, and I don't want anything to happen. That's why I'm glad you're here."

Hazel exchanged a look with Myrtle. Had Myrtle confided in Gloria about sending Hazel the note? What if Gloria was the one trying to kill her? "Myrtle told me about the path, the medicine mix-up, and was just starting to mention something about indigestion when you came in."

"That's right, the path was tampered with. I'm sure of it. Someone could've dug it out and placed those bricks back on top to disguise the tampering. I didn't even notice, and I was walking right with her." Gloria put her hand on top of Myrtle's. "And Auntie is very careful about her medicine. She knows how important that is."

"And what about the indigestion? Do you think someone is trying to poison her?"

"I'm afraid so." Gloria leaned forward. "It's no secret that Auntie is worth a lot of money, and I hate to say it, but most of my relatives would love to get their hands on it."

Hazel didn't mention that only a few seconds ago Myrtle had inferred that Gloria was in need of money. Was she one of those relatives? This was certainly a mystery that needed puzzling over, and Hazel wanted to retreat to her bedroom to think over the clues.

"What would you do next if this was in one of your novels?" Gloria asked.

Hazel stood up. "I guess I would first work out who had a motive. Then from those suspects I would narrow down who had the means and the opportunity to arrange these incidents."

Gloria snapped her fingers. "Of course. I think we already know the motive is most likely money. If Auntie were to die, Edward and Wes would benefit the most. Seems like either one of them would have had means and opportunity."

"Let's not jump to conclusions just yet. I'd like the chance to mull this over overnight if I may."

"Of course," Myrtle said.

Gloria patted the old woman's hand. "In the meantime, I'll stick close to you to ensure no one can make another attempt. I still haven't forgiven myself for being on holiday when your pills got mixed up, and I'm not going to let something else happen to you."

Hazel studied Gloria through narrowed eyes. Was the young woman truly as unselfishly devoted to Myrtle as she seemed, or was there something else going on?

"We'll talk more about this tomorrow." Hazel paused with her hand on the doorknob. "Maybe I can see this spot in the path that was tampered with for myself."

"Certainly," Myrtle said. "Tomorrow we're having some guests for afternoon tea and then badminton, croquet, and archery on the south lawn, but in the morning I'll be taking my constitutional as usual and will be walking right past that spot. You're welcome to join me."

"I'll do that." Hazel opened the door and exited into the hallway, her heart jumping in her chest as she came face to face with Fran, who practically had her ear pressed to the door.

FRAN JUMPED BACK IN SURPRISE, her wide eyes darting from Hazel to the door. "What were you doing in there with Grandmother?"

"Just catching up." Hazel's eyes fell on the cameo clasped at the neck of Fran's starched white blouse. "Were you going in to join us?" "

Fran's fingers flew up to the piece of jewelry. "I was going to see if Grandmother wanted hot chocolate, but I heard voices and wasn't sure if I should go in."

"It was just your grandmother, me, and Gloria in there. I'm sure you could go in."

Something flickered through Fran's eyes at the mention of Gloria's name, and Hazel hesitated. "Don't you like your cousin?"

"Second cousin," Fran corrected. "And I wouldn't trust her if I were you."

"Really? Why do you say that?"

"She's… been in trouble. That was a few years ago, but it's been a terrible strain on Grandmother. She acts like she's redeemed herself now, but I'm not sure…" Fran leaned closer to Hazel. "And she wasn't on any holiday the second week in July like she just said, either."

Hazel's eyes flicked to the door. So Fran *had* been eavesdropping. "How do you know that?"

"I saw her in town. Down on Fanuel Square. I normally wouldn't have remembered the exact date like that, but it was right before I was alerted by one of my nursing colleagues that Gram had taken sick from mixing up her pills."

Hadn't Myrtle just said Gloria was annoyed that she hadn't been called back from her holiday when the pill mix-up happened? But if Fran had seen her right before Myrtle took ill, then Gloria couldn't have been away.

"And did you speak with her? I thought she was on holiday."

Fran's eyes widened. "Oh no. I didn't speak with her. We're not on the best of terms." Her fingers came up to fiddle with the cameo again. A nervous habit? Hazel knew from her research that people often exhibited nervous habits when they were lying. Was Fran lying about running into Gloria? She did seem to have it in for the other girl, but *why* would she lie?

Hazel squinted at the cameo. Now that she was looking, she could see the shell cameo was extraordinary and unique, with a deeply carved scene of angels and cherubs and ringed with twinkling dark-red rubies. "I noticed your cameo matches the ring your grandmother wears."

Fran dropped her hand. "That's right. It's from a set of family heirloom jewelry."

"Did Myrtle give it to you?"

"Sort of. It came down from her grandmother, and some went to Gram and some to her sister, Enid. Then Gram gave some to Wes's mother and some to my father for my mother. It's been spread all over the family. It's not right, I tell you. A set like this should have stayed together and all gone to one person."

"Everyone in the family has a piece?"

"Some have more than one. Gloria has several because both her mother and her grandmother are gone. She inherited it all from that side." Fran's face fell. "I only have this."

Hazel squinted, trying to picture the Pembroke

family lineage. "So Gloria's grandmother was Myrtle's sister, and both her parents and grandparents are gone?"

Fran nodded. "I suppose that's why Gram dotes on her. Gram is the only family Gloria has left." Fran shrugged. "Vera has some cameos, too, because Wes's mother is dead, so her cameos were passed to Vera. Not that she would appreciate fine heirloom jewelry like this."

"No? She seems to like jewelry," Hazel said.

"They all do, but they have no sentiment. The cameos are valuable, but the only one in the family who appreciates the fact that they are family *heirlooms* is me."

It was obvious Fran thought she should be the keeper of the family cameos. And she clearly didn't like her relatives much. Hazel could tell she was the type to hold a grudge. But did Fran's attitude have anything to do with the attempts on Myrtle? Hazel couldn't think of any reason to connect the two. At least not yet.

She bid Fran good-bye, eager to get away from the sour young woman. The day had brought up many questions, and Hazel was eager to escape to her room and sort through them.

CHAPTER SIX

Hazel hurried down the hall toward the stairs, being careful to not make a sound. She could tell by the noises coming from the drawing room that the others were still up, but she wanted to go straight to her room. She needed to think about Myrtle's accidents, and she also had gleaned a great idea for her book based on the conversation in the library.

She slowly tiptoed up the stairs, not wanting a telltale creak to bring any of the family members out to delay her. She turned the corner to the hallway that led to her room, feeling relieved that she'd made it.

"*Merow!*"

"Dickens! What in the world are you doing out here?" Hazel peered down the hall toward her room.

The door was shut, but how had Dickens gotten out into the hall? Had someone been in her room?

Hazel open the door slowly and cautiously peered in. The room looked the same as she had left it. Dickens trotted in beside her and leapt onto the writing desk, looking at her expectantly. Surely if someone had been in her room, Dickens would alert her somehow?

"Well, where is it? Is there some sort of a secret panel?" She stood, hands on hips, staring at the cat. Dickens simply twitched his tail and started to wash his velvety brown face.

Hazel glanced around the room. The walls were nicely papered in a blue brocade. She didn't see any obvious panels. Maybe next to the fireplace? She made a quick round of the room, looking closely at the walls, but didn't see anything. Even if there was a panel, how would Dickens have opened it?

He must have gotten out some other way. Most likely when the maid had come in to tidy the room. It wouldn't be the first time he'd escaped that way.

Hazel glanced toward the bed and saw the vase on the side table had been refreshed with a new bunch of lilacs. Of course, that was what it was: the staff had been in to freshen up the room. Hazel felt relieved. She didn't like the idea of a secret passage where anyone could sneak into the room. And she also didn't like the idea of Dickens being able to run free around the house.

"Dickens, you bad boy. You know you're supposed to stay in the room. If you want to venture outside, we will have to use the harness."

Hazel rummaged in her trunk, pulling out the contraption that Lord Wallingford had given to her. It was a modified collar that acted as a harness that went around the legs and across the back. Dickens hated it. Whenever she tried to force him to wear it, he simply flopped down on the ground and refused to move. She wiggled it in front of him now, and he backed up and hissed at the despicable object. "I won't make you wear it now, but I'm warning you, you'd better stay in this room, or else."

Dickens glared at her for a few seconds then hopped up on the desk, sitting on the edge with the tip of his tail tapping slightly on her notebook.

"I know. I know. I need to get writing." She pulled out the chair and sat then selected the Sheaffer pen from her lineup. But she didn't start writing. She wasn't quite ready for that yet. Tapping the end of the pen on her lips, she closed her eyes, sorting through everything she'd learned since coming to Lowry House.

Did someone really want Myrtle dead, or were the incidents just accidents? Myrtle's relatives certainly were a strange lot, but murder was a very serious crime, and Myrtle was already eighty. She did seem to be in very good health, but why would someone risk getting caught when they need only wait a few years for Myrtle to die naturally?

Maybe someone had a reason to want her dead right away. Of course, that could be many things. They might need money desperately, or Myrtle might know something that they don't want her to tell. Or maybe the person was just so angry about something that doing Myrtle in was more of an obsession.

"*Mew.*" Dickens blinked his cobalt-blue eyes at her.

"So you think the killer is doing it out of emotion?" Hazel rubbed Dickens behind the ears. He tilted his head to the right in order to take full advantage. Thoughts of Fran came to mind. The girl did seem angry. She was obviously put out that she wasn't the keeper of the family cameos. But why would she vent her frustrations on Myrtle? Myrtle wasn't responsible for dispersing the cameos in the first place; Myrtle's parents were.

Maybe in Fran's warped mind she thought her father, being the only male in the family, should have inherited the entire lot of them. But if Myrtle were to die, to whom would she leave the cameos currently in her possession?

Was Fran strong enough to have dug out the path herself? Hazel would have to assess that tomorrow. Myrtle had said no one was at the house the day her pills got mixed up, but Fran could have sneaked in. By her own admission, she was here quite soon, having heard about it from an associate.

And what was that bit about Fran seeing Gloria in town when she was supposed to be on vacation? Why would Fran not speak to her cousin if she saw her, especially to convey the news that Myrtle was ill? What kind of trouble had Gloria been in, *and* was she still in it?

But if Gloria was the one trying to kill Myrtle, wouldn't she be trying to convince everyone the incidents were truly accidents? She was doing the opposite. Earlier in the library, she had acted more convinced than Myrtle herself that someone was trying to harm her.

"*Meropp.*" Dickens stretched his long body.

"I know," Hazel said. "One can't go by what they see on the surface. One has to dig deeper. And I do get the sneaking suspicion that Gloria is hiding something. Myrtle mentioned that Gloria doesn't have a lot of money, and the two of them are close. Perhaps Myrtle is leaving her something in the will, and Gloria doesn't want to wait for her to die in order to get it."

Dickens hopped down from the desk and trotted over to the bed then pawed down the corner of the silky covers under which Hazel had tucked her light cotton nightgown.

"That's right, I should change… Wait… *change*. What if Myrtle was about to change her will? *That* would be a reason to kill her now instead of waiting for her to die naturally."

Dickens didn't react to Hazel's brilliant deduction. He simply curled into a ball on her pillow and buried his face in his tail.

"If that were the case," Hazel continued, "any one of the relatives might want to stop her. Maybe she was going to *include* Gloria? Then Wes and Edward wouldn't get as much money."

Thoughts of Wes and Vera surfaced. They were already benefiting from Myrtle's generosity by living in the cottage.

Hazel's eyes flicked to the window, where a dim yellow light shone in the distance. Was that the cottage? She vaguely remembered a stone caretaker's dwelling somewhere along the edge of the estate.

Near enough for someone to sneak into the house and tamper with Myrtle's medicines then sneak back out without anyone knowing. Also close enough to dig out the path in the middle of the night and sneak back into the cottage unseen. And, obviously, they must need money, or else they wouldn't be living in the cottage, though judging by Vera's appearance, she had plenty to spend on clothes and jewelry, not to mention nail polish and makeup.

Hadn't Myrtle mentioned something about indigestion? Myrtle had put it off, thinking it wasn't unusual for someone of her age to have indigestion, but Gloria had thought it had a more sinister meaning. Could someone be slowly poisoning Myrtle? If so, they would need frequent access to her food.

Hazel's gaze flicked from the window to her research notebook. Ironically, poison was the very thing she was writing about, and she had the research fresh in her memory. There were plenty of poisons, especially natural ones, that would mimic indigestion. Maybe someone was peppering Myrtle's food with something that would build up in her system and eventually prove fatal.

And what about Edward? He coveted the fine antiques in the house. Maybe Edward felt that he should be getting some of them now and was harboring a long-time resentment against his mother. Maybe he was jealous that Wes got to live in the cottage for free while his own daughter, Fran, had to fend for herself in town.

Hopefully, Hazel would be able to narrow things down further tomorrow. She knew from her books that figuring out the motive was a good path to finding the killer—or, in this case, attempted killer.

Unless Myrtle was blackmailing someone or knew a terrible secret, or someone was so angry they wanted the satisfaction of killing her, the motive was most likely money. Tomorrow, Hazel would find out the specifics of Myrtle's will, if she planned to make any changes, and if anyone would be afraid of anything she knew.

She could also inquire delicately about Gloria's trouble. The wording Fran had used alluded to her having straightened out, which made Hazel think perhaps it had something to do with drugs. She certainly hoped not. Gloria seemed like such a nice girl, and she doted on Myrtle, and obviously Myrtle cared for her. But if Gloria was mixed up with drugs, she might need money badly. Badly enough to kill Myrtle?

At the same time, she could find out the story about Wes. Did he work? How long had he had a drinking problem, and what exactly was his financial situation? From Charles's long career at Scotland Yard, she knew that drinking often went along with drugs and gambling. Had Wes gotten involved with something like that? If so, he might need money badly, too.

Hazel hated the idea of having to dig into Myrtle's family's personal secrets, but Myrtle had asked her to help, and there was no other way. Once she had those answers, it would hopefully shed some light on who might be behind all of this. Because right now, from where she was sitting, it could be just about anyone.

Hazel flipped open her notebook. Myrtle had inadvertently given her an idea for the book. She'd noticed that Myrtle had been trying to cover up some of her forgetfulness. Even though it was only natural for someone of her age, and since Myrtle was so vibrant and full of life, Hazel could see why she would work hard to cover up those sporadic memory lapses… maybe even fooling herself into thinking she wasn't having them. She knew Myrtle really was having memory problems, but the thought occurred to her that she could use it in the opposite way in her novel and cause the killer to cover up by only *pretending* to have memory problems.

Uncapping her pen, she bent over the book, excitement welling up inside her. She'd always had Charles to bounce ideas off for her plots and to help her fill in the details. She'd been blocked on coming up with the first big twist in her novel, worried she wouldn't be able to do it without Charles. But now she had it. She'd come up with it on her own, and some of the details of the murder—at least the one in her novel—were finally coming together.

CHAPTER SEVEN

The next morning at breakfast, Hazel found herself considering everyone at the table with renewed suspicion. The best china from the previous night's dinner had been washed and was now on display in an oak china cabinet. Next to the cabinet, the breakfast was set out buffet-style atop a long server. White bone-china plates with a thin silver rim were stacked next to the stainless steel chafing dishes.

Vera sat at the table with half a piece of toast on her plate. The seat next to her was empty, as if announcing Wes's absence. Across the table from her, Gloria had a plate loaded with bacon, eggs, .

Myrtle was in great spirits, drinking tea and picking at a plate of prunes. Fran stuck to toast, dabbing a tiny teaspoon of marmalade on top and topping it off with tea and milk. Hazel put a small pile of scrambled eggs on her plate, added a thin slice of bread, and joined them at the table.

"The staff is setting up the games on the lawn today, and more guests will arrive after noon for tea and play." Myrtle's blue eyes sparkled with excitement. She didn't seem the least bit worried that someone might be trying to kill her. Had she forgotten already? Hazel knew Myrtle was having memory issues, but this morning, she appeared to be sharp as a tack.

"I just hope someone doesn't walk away with the expensive stuff. You know what happened to the Rothingtons." Edward reached for the gleaming silver teapot in the middle of the table, lifting it up and then ducking his head to look at the bottom. "Oh, Mother, this is a Birmingham set. Honestly, you should put this away. It's quite valuable and should not be for daily use."

Myrtle waved her hand in the air. "*Pffft...* What good are these nice things if we can't use them?"

"These are fine antiques. They should be preserved for future generations."

Hazel's eyes narrowed. By "future generations," did Edward mean himself? Myrtle was incredibly wealthy, but what was Edward's financial status? He was a fairly well-known antiques dealer, but did he have money of his own? Just because Myrtle had money didn't mean she gave it out to her children. Many people didn't… at least not while they were alive. And Edward would be in a perfect position to know the exact value of everything he would eventually inherit.

"What happened to the Rothingtons?" Hazel asked.

Myrtle waved her hand. "Oh, that was so long ago. Really, it was nothing. A little robbery at one of their parties."

"I'm sure Vera would remember." Edward shot Vera a pointed look.

Hazel's brows rose. Was Edward accusing Vera of stealing from the Rothingtons? He didn't seem to be overly fond of his nephew's wife, but then it wasn't like he and Wes seemed that close either.

She studied Vera out of the corner of her eye, but the woman seemed nonplussed by the accusation. She sat calmly, nibbling on her toast. Today, her hair appeared even brighter red, and she had on even more lipstick, but what really caught Hazel's eye was the large red rectangular pendant that sparkled like it had been electrified at her throat. It must've been synthetic, as Hazel doubted Vera could afford a ruby of that size. Odd that she wouldn't wear the family cameo jewelry. Then again, maybe she felt it was too old-fashioned for her modern look.

Myrtle pushed her plate away and dabbed her lips with her ivory linen napkin. "Well, that was delicious, but I'm ready for my morning constitutional." She turned to Hazel with a knowing look. "Would you care to join me?"

"I'd be delighted." Hazel bid farewell to everyone else, and the two women strolled out onto the lawn, with Myrtle pointing out various plantings as they made their way through the garden beside the house and on to the brick path.

The sun warmed Hazel's shoulders, and the smell of freshly mown grass tickled her nose. She could hear people running about the grounds, most likely setting things up for the afternoon's events. Blue tits twittered in the perfectly manicured trees, and squirrels scampered through the shrubbery, which had been pruned in twisty conical shapes.

"It must be quite a chore to keep up the garden like this." Hazel's garden at Hastings Manor was not nearly as grand as this one, and her gardener was kept quite busy with it.

"Oh, it is. We employ several full-time gardeners. My parents always prided themselves on their large gardens, and I can't imagine it any other way," Myrtle said.

"Interesting that you, and not your sister, inherited the house," Hazel said. "Was that a problem between you two?"

"Oh, not at all," Myrtle said. "Enid didn't want the house or anything. She wanted money." Myrtle's face turned sad, and she slowed her step. "You see, Enid had a gambling problem. I tried to help her, but she refused the help. So it ended up being a good thing I inherited the house, as she would've lost it. She lost everything she had in the end."

"Oh, that's so sad… but what about her daughter? That would be Gloria's mother, am I right?"

Myrtle nodded. "Yes. Her name was Rose. I helped them as much as I could, but Rose was very proud. She didn't want to take help. And Gloria is just like her."

"So you don't give Gloria money?"

"Not now."

"But you did?"

"Well, not money outright." Myrtle lowered her voice and leaned toward Hazel. "Gloria hasn't had it easy. With the way Enid lost the money, and Rose, well, she somewhat followed in her mother's footsteps. Gloria didn't have much of a chance. Anyway, Gloria fell in with the wrong crowd, and she had a problem with drugs. I helped her."

"Oh, but she seems so... well put together," Hazel said. So *that* was the trouble Fran had referred to.

"She is now. She's been clean for ages. I'm sure you can tell I'm quite fond of the girl. Everyone in the family is. Why, she even introduced Vera and Wes years ago."

Hazel frowned. "Gloria and Vera are friends?" Hazel hadn't noticed them acting like old friends, and she considered herself somewhat of an observer of human nature... it was a trait that made her books more realistic.

"Yes. Back when she was... well, years ago."

If Gloria knew Vera from years ago, did Vera also have a drug problem? And if so, did she need money for it? It was obvious Wes had a problem with

alcohol, and while Hazel had been under the impression the drinking had started when Sarah died, maybe it had more to do with his wife's influence than his mother's death.

"I can see you're very fond of Gloria."

"I'm proud of what she's overcome," Myrtle added. "She's very strong. I worry sometimes about what will happen to her after I'm gone. She still has a little money in a trust that her grandmother managed to leave behind. Thankfully, she didn't spend that on the drugs. And she's frugal. Doesn't spend it on expensive clothing and jewelry. But if the money ran out, I suppose she'd need to acquire a position to get by. You know, a secretarial job or the like."

"You're not going to leave her any money?" Hazel asked then, at Myrtle's strange look, added, "I need to ask about your will to figure out who might be trying to harm you."

"Oh, right. You think someone wants to kill me for my money?"

"Well, that could be one reason. It happens quite often."

Myrtle chuckled. "I'm sure it does. But if that's the case, then it's not Gloria. I considered including her, but I guess I'm rather old-fashioned, and it didn't seem fair to Wes and Edward. I always intended for everything to be split equally between my children, Sarah and Edward. But now that Sarah has passed, Wes would get her share.

"If I included something for Gloria, I'm sure Fran's nose would be out of joint since Gloria really isn't technically one of my own family. In the end, I decided it was best to keep things to my immediate children or their issue, so Gloria's not in my will at all."

"Really? And are the terms of your will common knowledge?"

"Oh yes, everyone knows that all I have will be split equally between Edward and Wes." Myrtle stepped over a gnarled root that had heaved up the bricks and then glanced back at it. "I'll have to tell Dooley to tend to that."

"And you weren't talking about changing your will at all? How old is your current will?"

Myrtle shook her head. "No changes. The last change was shortly after Sarah died, so it's about ten years old now."

That narrowed things down. Gloria didn't appear to still have a drug problem, but Hazel had noticed her clothing was well worn. She clearly didn't have a lot. It seemed like Gloria would benefit more from Myrtle being alive. Myrtle helped her out now, and after she was dead, all her money would be in the hands of Wes and Edward. Hazel doubted either of them would help Gloria like Myrtle did. No wonder Gloria was so concerned about the accidents.

"Tell me about Wes and Vera. I know you let them live in the cottage. Don't they have any means of support?"

Myrtle sighed. "Poor Wes. He was always such a sensitive boy. Hasn't been the same since his mother died. Never knew his father, you know, so Sarah was all he had. It was awfully tragic the way she was killed in that car accident…"

Myrtle's voice drifted off, and Hazel felt a pang of guilt for churning up old, painful memories. She couldn't imagine what it was like to lose a child, but the pain of losing someone who was close never went away, as Hazel knew very well herself. Unfortunately, it was necessary to ask these questions to get to the bottom of things.

"Is that when his drinking started?" Hazel asked.

"Yes. Wes isn't terribly strong. He's always needed something… some kind of crutch to carry him through. After Sarah died, I was terribly worried about his mental state. But things got a little better when he met Vera. He was a promising pianist, but Sarah's death seemed to have bled all the creativity out of him. Naturally, I offered him the cottage while he recovers."

"And how long has he been there?"

"Oh, about seven years now."

Hazel doubted that Wes was going to make a recovery after seven years, but she didn't want to say so. What would be the point? But now she had to wonder if Wes was the one trying to kill Myrtle. He would get even more money after Myrtle died, and not have to scrape away in an old cottage. And if Wes didn't care about money, then Vera certainly did. By the looks of things, she liked to be kept in the latest fashions... and that cost money.

"Well, at least Edward has done well for himself," Hazel prompted. Maybe she could knock him off the list of suspects, too.

"He does all right. He has a little country house. Not anything grand like this." Myrtle gestured back toward the house.

"Does he ever come to you for money?" Hazel asked.

Myrtle pressed her lips together. "No. Sometimes he does ask about an item around the house, but I assume that's purely because he loves antiques."

Or loves what he can sell them for. Hazel decided to keep that thought to herself.

"And Fran? What does she do?"

"She's a nurse's aide. Studying to be a nurse."

"And she's not in your will at all?"

"No. But I suppose she might benefit through Edward. He would inherit half the items in the house and might give some to her."

"I noticed Fran seems to be quite enamored with the family cameo she wears."

"She is. I have to say she is a strange girl, even if she is my granddaughter. To be honest, I get on better with Gloria." Myrtle looked down at her ring. "Gloria, Vera, and Fran all have cameo brooches. I have several other cameo pieces. Earrings, necklaces, bracelets. They are divided amongst Wes and Edward in my will, so I imagine Edward would give his to Fran." Myrtle jerked her head up to look at Hazel. "But surely you don't think she'd kill me over cameos?"

Hazel put a reassuring hand on Myrtle's arm. "It's unlikely. We don't even know if someone actually *is* trying to kill you."

"That's right. I wouldn't have even thought a thing, until Gloria said things added up to be suspicious. I told Gloria it was coincidence... but she seems to think otherwise. I just don't think it could be one of my family." Myrtle hooked her arm through Hazel's. "That's why it's such a good thing you dropped by. Now you can work out what is really going on."

Hazel felt a twinge of anxiety. Myrtle was putting her confidence in her, and she hoped she'd be up to the task of getting to the bottom of these coincidental "accidents."

"Does Vera have a job?"

Myrtle snorted. "Lord, no! That girl wouldn't soil her hands with work."

"And you said Wes gave her Sarah's cameos and anything else he got from her, is that right?"

Myrtle made a face. "As if Vera would even care about cameos or Sarah's old jewelry. I think they are too old-fashioned for her."

Myrtle pulled up short, tugging Hazel back a step, then unlinked her arm and pointed at the path. "This is the area of the path that was washed out, right here."

Hazel stopped to inspect the path. It was cut into a steep hill, sweeping upward to the left and then falling off dramatically to the right. It was obvious where the gardener had made the repair. Hazel squatted down to get a better look at the earth around it, wishing she'd thought to bring a small gardening spade.

She clawed at the dirt, trying to ascertain how difficult the digging would be. She didn't care that the brown earth became lodged under her fingernails. Her fingers were already splotched with ink, and besides, people expected her to be a little unusual. The ground was thick with roots, just as Myrtle had said earlier. It would have been hard work, but someone could have dug it out with a spade that had a sharp, thin blade. She pried up a brick to look at the roots to see if there had been a clean break made from a blade, or more of a twisty break made from nature. She saw both but then realized the clean breaks could have been made when the gardener had dug it out to repair.

Someone certainly could have removed the dirt under the bricks on purpose and then replaced them in such a way that the ground underneath was not so solid. Hazel scrambled down the side of the hill a few feet. Sure enough, there were some round rocks that didn't seem natural for that spot. What if someone had dug out the dirt under the bricks and put a few small round rocks and then the bricks on top. It would appear as if the bricks were solidly in the path, but when one stepped on the brick, the rocks underneath would make it roll out from under foot and could cause a nasty spill. The kind of spill that could be fatal for an elderly person if they landed on their head.

Myrtle was looking at her with concern. "So what's the verdict?"

"I don't know. Someone could have done this on purpose. But I can't tell who. It would've been hard to dig. A man could have done it, or a strong woman could have done it with both hands on the shovel."

Hazel looked back down the path, shading her eyes from the sun. From where they stood, the house was not visible. This spot in the path was secluded by trees and shrubbery and the hill. It wouldn't have been hard to dig it up without being seen.

"You say you walk this path every day?" Hazel asked.

"Unless the weather does not comply or I don't feel good."

"Then if someone did take this out, they did it in between the time you last walked it and the time you fell. Who would've been here the night or morning before you went on your walk?"

"Well, that doesn't narrow it down. Everyone was here. I tripped on Monday. The day before was Sunday, and that's the day we all gather for family dinner in the afternoon, so they were all here after I took my walk."

CHAPTER EIGHT

H azel grew quiet as they continued on the path, which wound around a garden of wild-flowers riotous with color then turned back toward the house. Had someone really tampered with the bricks? If that was the case, then Myrtle really *was* in danger. What if someone right this minute was planning their next attempt on Myrtle's life?

Gloria came trotting up behind them. "Did you show her the spot in the path?"

"Yes, we're just on our way back now," Myrtle said.

"So what do you think?" Gloria's eyes flicked from Hazel, back down the path toward the spot. "Do you think someone did this on purpose?"

Hazel's heart twisted at the look of fear that crossed Myrtle's face. Apparently she wasn't as blasé about this whole thing as she would have one believe. "It could have been done on purpose. But there's no way to tell for sure."

"I knew it!" Gloria put her arm around Myrtle's shoulders. "Now will you listen to me? You need to be careful."

"I don't know. Even if someone did dig out the path, it's unlikely that one little trip on bricks would kill me. Seems like a silly plan if someone wanted to do me in," Myrtle pointed out.

"I'm just glad I was there when you tripped. Otherwise, the damage could have been much worse. You might have hit your head, and that can be very dangerous," Gloria said.

Myrtle rapped her head lightly with her knuckles. "It's going to take a lot more than a bump on the head to put this old lady out of commission."

"I hope so." Gloria slid her eyes over to Hazel. "Do you have any suspects?"

"Nothing concrete. You know one has to be very careful before they start naming people, and we're not really sure exactly what is going on. Do you have any idea who it might be?"

Gloria chewed her bottom lip, her eyes darting over to the edge of the estate in the direction of the cottage. Was she trying to say she thought it was Wes?

Then she looked down at the ground. "It wouldn't be right to say."

"Indeed. That would be a serious accusation," Myrtle said.

"This *is* serious. Did you tell her everything?" Gloria asked Myrtle. "The path, the poisoning, and the medicines?"

"She did," Hazel answered for Myrtle. "I've seen the path, and someone *could* have tampered with it, but the medicine mix-up could have just been due to Myrtle getting confused about which pills were which, and the poisoning... well, honestly, that just sounds like indigestion. Maybe the path really was washed out or it was a one-time attempt and nothing more is going to happen."

They had come to the end of the brick walkway and were looking over an expanse of lush green lawn. To the right, the edge of a koi pond peeked out from behind an enormous rose garden. From their vantage point atop a slightly sloping hill, there was a sweeping view of much of the estate to the left. Hazel could see that badminton nets, archery targets, and croquet hoops had already been set up.

"These things are no accident," Gloria said. "Auntie is very careful with her medicines. And the indigestion, well, I don't need to tell you, Hazel, that there are several poisons that build up in one's system and kill you over time. Auntie never had indigestion until recently."

Hazel chewed her bottom lip. It was true, natural herbs such as white snake root—the very herb rumored to have killed Abraham Lincoln's mother—were known to build up to toxic levels over time. And then there were poisons that caused bodily functions to go awry, killing you not with the poison itself but with what it did to your insides.

Hazel didn't want to think about that. Myrtle ate much the same foods as everyone else, and if someone was putting poison in them, might they be putting it in the dishes everyone was eating? She made a mental note to see if anyone avoided certain dishes at dinner.

"When the medicines were switched, it wasn't the day of your usual Sunday dinner, was it?" Hazel asked.

"No. It was a Tuesday," Myrtle said. She appeared to be sharp as a tack now. Hazel hadn't seen any of the hazy memory issues that she'd noticed yesterday. Maybe it came and went. The question was, had she been having memory issues on Tuesday, and had those issues caused her to take the wrong medicine?

"That's right. I remember you said the doctor was at his club." Hazel turned to Gloria. "Now, Myrtle said you were away, so you didn't know who was at the house that day, is that correct?"

"That's right. I was angry as anything when I came back. Someone should've sent a telegram or sent Giles for me or something."

"Nonsense!" Myrtle said. "Why ruin a great holiday? And you would have wasted money on the room at Gull Landing if you'd just up and left. Besides, I was fine. The doctor said I would have to have taken a lot more pills for something dire to happen."

"You stayed at Gull Landing?" Hazel asked.

Gloria's cheeks blushed pink. "I don't have much money and couldn't afford a big expensive hotel."

"Oh, but that's a lovely place. One doesn't need a grand hotel to have a good time on holiday." Hazel didn't want to embarrass the girl about her lack of finances, and even though she made oodles of money with her books, she did truly believe that you didn't need money to be happy.

Gloria turned to Myrtle. "Are you going in now?"

Myrtle looked toward the rose garden, her lips curling into a smile. "I think I'll sit in the arbor. I want to show Hazel the various rose species. Will you join us?"

Gloria touched Myrtle's arm lightly. "I'd love to, but I have to talk to Cook about the refreshments and make sure she's set for the party. You have a nice time, though, and be careful. Even though some of these incidents can be explained, I still think you might be in danger." Gloria flicked Hazel a knowing look and then started back toward the house.

"Well, she certainly is a worrywart, isn't she?" Myrtle grabbed Hazel's arm and propelled her toward the rose garden. "As I told you earlier, my mother loved these gardens. And she loved the roses in particular. Did you know that she grew many rare varieties?"

"No. They certainly are beautiful." A large arched entryway covered with climbing pink roses heralded the entrance to the rose garden. Inside, there were roses of every color. Red, white, yellow, pink, and even many whose petals had more than one color. There were rose trees, rose bushes, and lattice-work with climbing rose vines everywhere. Myrtle took delight in describing the different species: flori-bunda, English garden roses, Portlands, and grandi-flora. Hazel had had no idea there were so many different varieties. Fuzzy yellow-and-black bumble-bees buzzed around the plants as Myrtle led her to a white bench canopied by an arched arbor of gigantic papery white tea roses.

They sat next to each other on the bench. From here, the view of the pond was striking. The canopy of the rose-laden arbor shielded the bench from view on all sides except directly in front. A secret resting spot where one could only be seen from one section of the property. Hazel settled in, leaning her head against the back of the bench while she listened to the buzz of the bees and drank in the papery floral scent of the roses. "You're lucky to have Gloria looking out for you."

"Indeed." Myrtle turned a sharp eye in her direction. "She has nothing to do with these attacks... if that is even what they are."

"I hope she has nothing to gain by hurting you, and if it wasn't for her, you might have been more severely injured when you fell on the path." Hazel mentally crossed Gloria off the suspect list. Even though she sensed the girl was keeping something back. It was more likely she was embarrassed that Hazel might find out about her background with drugs. Hazel hadn't seen any evidence of recent drug indulgence with the girl. In fact, the hearty breakfast Gloria had eaten that morning, the clear look in her eyes, and the strength of her voice indicated she truly had given them up.

"She's a good girl. She's not mixed up with that crowd anymore," Myrtle said as if reading her mind.

"Yes, she seems it. So she doesn't associate with anyone from her drug days?"

"Oh, no. And it's a good thing, too. Those people were bad influences, and with that nasty scandal, a few are in prison."

"prison?"

"Yes, the robbery at the Rothingtons' about five years back. They did it for money to buy drugs." Myrtle sneaked a look at Hazel. "Gloria wasn't involved in that, of course!"

"Of course." Maybe Gloria hadn't been involved, but what about Vera? Gloria had known Vera back then. "Are Gloria and Vera good friends? They don't seem very chummy, from what I've seen."

Myrtle scratched at her face. "I don't know if they were close friends, but they mixed with the same crowd, and that's how Wes met Vera."

"Did Wes and Vera also have drug problems?"

Myrtle looked at her sharply and leaned forward in her seat. "Not Wes. His vice has always been alcohol. Now Vera, I don't really know, but I've never seen her look drugged. You don't think Wes and Vera would try to hurt me, do you? Honestly, I'm beginning to wonder if anyone really is trying to hurt me. All these events seem to have logical explanations."

Hazel had been wondering about that herself. Not only did the incidents have logical explanations, they didn't seem drastic enough to kill Myrtle. Unless the killer wasn't thinking straight, like someone under the influence of drugs or alcohol might be.

But then Myrtle herself had written for her to come, so she must have thought someone was trying to harm her. "Myrtle, you must have your suspicions. Your letter said as well. Surely you must have a suspicion. Do you have any enemies or maybe have information that someone else might not want others to find out about?"

Myrtle looked at her in confusion. "I certainly don't have any enemies or secrets to tell. And I don't know of any—"

Thwack!

Hazel stared in horror at the arrow that had whizzed in front of her face and embedded itself in the latticework less than an inch from Myrtle's head.

CHAPTER NINE

The iridescent blue feathered end quivered in front of Myrtle's shocked face, the razor-sharp arrow point piercing one of the roses almost dead center.

"Are you all right?" Hazel sprang up from the bench as she asked the question, barely waiting for Myrtle's nod before taking off in the direction from which the arrow was shot.

Hazel lurched down the path toward the exit of the rose garden. A thorn snagged the bottom of her dress and she hesitated only to pull it loose. Maggie would probably fuss over the torn lace, but she couldn't worry about that now.

She careened out of the arbor, looking around for anyone who might help her give chase, but she did not see a soul. Turning quickly to look back at the bench in order to determine from which angle the arrow would've been shot, she realized the shooter would've been standing to the left. She headed in that direction, barreling toward a copse of thick trees.

Had the arrow simply been an unlucky shot gone astray from someone practicing the targets? But no one was here for the games yet. Had one of the staff been testing it out? She whirled around again, looking at the angles, but it was impossible. The targets were not anywhere near the bench. Not to mention that the shooter would be looking to retrieve the arrow.

She hesitated at the trees, squinting into the woods and straining her ears to hear the sound of someone running. But she did not see or hear anyone. Should she venture in? She took one step forward and almost stepped on the brown wooden archer's bow lying just beside the narrow path that led into the woods. She bent down to pick it up, her heart thudding when she saw what was lying beside it. An arrow with iridescent blue feathers exactly like the one that had almost skewered Myrtle.

Her gaze flicked to the woods. Had the shooter escaped down this path? Why else would the bow and arrow be lying here? But why throw it down in the first place?

Hazel hesitated only a second before heading into

the dark woods. Myrtle's life was at stake, and if someone had just shot an arrow at her and run off into these woods, then Hazel needed to find them.

The woods felt dark and menacing compared to the cheery midmorning sunshine Hazel had been enjoying in the rose garden. As she made her way farther into the woods, the hair on the back of her neck stood up as if someone were watching. She whirled around, but no one was there.

That's the trouble with having a writer's vivid imagination. Hazel pushed all her dark thoughts away and focused on the cheery twitter of the birds instead.

Squirrels scampered on the ground and gathered nuts. A blue jay flew between the branches of the tall pines, letting out a raucous cry. The animals of the forest were going about their usual business as if a potential killer had not just run through.

The path wasn't long, and soon she saw a bright, sunlit clearing. The path led right to the stone cottage. It was exactly as she remembered from her visits here when she was younger. Was this the cottage that Wes and Vera lived in now?

She stood at the edge of the woods, hidden by a big pine tree, afraid to venture out. Was it Wes or Vera who had shot the arrow at Myrtle? Or had someone else run into the woods and taken refuge in the cottage or maybe even taken a different path? Voices drifted out from the cottage. She was too far away to hear the words, but she could tell the voices were shrill with anger.

She crept along the edge of the tree line to get closer without having to expose herself in the clearing. If the killer was out there, she didn't want them to know she had been chasing them.

Now she could distinguish the arguing voices. It was a man and a woman. Wes and Vera.

"…Maybe you should think about getting a job instead of sleeping half the time and wandering around the estate," the woman said.

"Job? My family provides for the roof over your head. Maybe you should curtail all the spending … not to mention your excursions … and we'd have more money to go around."

"Excursions? How would you even know when I've gone out or not? You're always in a drunken stupor. If you were a real man—"

"Real man! Is that what you're doing when you sneak out? If I catch you with another man, it will be the last time—"

"Let go of me! And don't threaten me ever again!"

A door slammed. Hazel shrank back behind a

tree. The last thing she needed was for one of them to catch her overhearing their argument. Especially if that person was the same person who was orchestrating the attempts on Myrtle's life.

But if Vera or Wes had been the shooter, how could they have had enough time to run back here and get into an argument? Hazel had given chase immediately. Unless the argument had started when that person rushed in after shooting the arrow. Hazel supposed that could be the case. She hadn't heard enough to know how long the argument had been going on for.

Or maybe Vera and Wes had planned this together, and the argument was an act. An alibi in case someone came rushing here after the arrow was shot.

Hazel hurried back toward the rose garden, the bow weighing heavy in her hand. If she'd had any doubts that someone was trying to kill Myrtle before, she hadn't any now. It was extremely unlikely that the arrow was a shot gone astray. So, therefore, it seemed they did indeed have a killer in their midst.

Myrtle was still seated on the bench. Fran had joined her. The arrow still stuck out from the side of the arbor.

"Did you find them?" Myrtle asked.

"No." Hazel held up the bow and arrow.

"What's going on here?" Fran pointed to the arrow. "Did someone shoot at you?"

Myrtle slid a glance at Hazel, and she shook her head slightly. It wouldn't do to have Fran thinking they knew someone was trying to harm Myrtle.

Myrtle patted Fran's arm. "Oh, don't be silly. It was probably just a stray arrow. Someone testing the equipment."

"But the targets are way over there…" Fran gestured toward the far side of the estate then swiveled her head to look at Myrtle and then back to Hazel. "You don't think someone shot it here on purpose, do you?"

"Of course not." Hazel tugged at the arrow, but it was embedded in the wood. She planted her feet for leverage and tried again. "This thing is in there good."

"Let me." Fran stood and pulled the arrow out easily. The rose it had pierced fell to the ground in a flurry of petals.

"I must have loosened it for you," Hazel said.

"They can get stuck in good. I'm pretty strong, though, from my nursing studies. Takes a lot of strength to do nursing. A lot of people don't realize that. I like to keep myself fit by helping around in the gardens. I even made a little kitchen garden for Wes. He loves fresh vegetables, and I planted all kinds of herbs and easy vegetables like tomatoes and cucumbers. Not that Vera cooks much." Fran's mouth turned down in disapproval at the mention of Vera not cooking. She handed the arrow to Hazel. "Are you sure you're okay, Gram? That landed pretty near. What happened?"

"Hazel and I were just sitting here, and *thwap*. It sailed by and lodged there, nearly an inch from my head." She patted her hair. "Nearly ruined my coif."

Fran turned to look at Hazel. "Gram hasn't been feeling well lately, and she seems to be a little… confused. You know there was an incident with the medicine and… well, one could hardly blame her at her age. I have plenty of patients who mixed up their pills."

"I know. It can be scary to have such a close call. But all is well." Hazel gave Myrtle a look over Fran's head. She didn't want anyone to know their suspicions. From Hazel's vast experience, she knew it was better to let the potential killer think they were going to get away with murder. They would be easier to catch when they thought no one was on to them. The fewer people who knew she suspected someone was trying to kill Myrtle, the better.

Myrtle laughed. "Yes, of course. Just a silly accident."

"Oh, that's good." Fran stood up. "Well, I'm glad it came to no harm. I would hate to think of someone shooting at the two of you. Well, now, I'm going in to freshen up before people start to arrive."

Hazel watched Fran. Once she was out of earshot, Myrtle said, "That was a close call. But I don't understand one thing."

"What's that?" Hazel asked.

"Why would someone risk shooting at me when you were sitting right beside me? Surely they would've known that you'd give chase."

Good question. Hazel stepped back from the bench. The way it was situated, one could only see the bench head-on from across the pond, where there was a densely wooded area far from the house. No one had been over there that Hazel had noticed. The bench was obscured from most other angles by the lush rosebushes and junipers growing in the garden. The arbor canopy over the bench itself was full of blooms and dense with leaves, so that only one corner of the bench was visible from the house. The corner Myrtle had sat on. The side Hazel had sat on would've been obscured by the roses. And that was exactly the direction from which the arrow had been shot.

"Did you say that you sit on this bench every day?" Hazel asked.

"Yes. It's part of my morning walk. I walk the garden path and then end up sitting here alone. I like the time to reflect on things. Everyone knows that."

"Exactly. Everyone knows that go for your morning walk and everyone knew I accompanied you. But they also know that you like to sit here *alone*. No one knew that I also accompanied you to the garden. The only person who knew that was was Gloria."

"And the archery targets being set up offer a perfect opportunity for this to look like an accident." Myrtle completed Hazel's grim thought.

"When I leaped from the bench in pursuit, I must've surprised them. They might have thought they had all the time in the world to stage it as an accident. Or perhaps their initial plan was to shoot the arrow off, thinking to incriminate someone else." Hazel glanced at the bow. Did the fact that it was found on the path to Wes and Vera's cottage lead to one of them being the shooter, or was it dropped there on purpose?

Wes's judgement was impaired by alcohol, but if

he was the shooter, wouldn't he have just taken the bow back to the cottage and hidden it? Unless he knew Vera was at home and didn't want her to see him with it. It was clear from their argument that the lack of finances was affecting their marriage. Maybe Wes had become desperate to get his hands on Myrtle's money right away.

But she didn't want to voice that suspicion to Myrtle. She needed physical proof before she named anyone, and she knew from Charles's cases and her own mystery novels that oftentimes things were not as they seemed.

"I do hope we don't need to call in the police," Myrtle said nervously. "I'd rather handle this within the family. Find out whoever is doing this and put a stop to it… hopefully before they're successful."

"There's nothing really to call them in for. No crime has been committed, and unfortunately, they won't act solely on our suspicions. We really have no proof to offer them."

"If only you'd been able to catch the person." Myrtle looked wistfully toward the edge of the garden. "Funny, though. It's so quiet and peaceful here, you'd think we would've seen or heard whoever shot the arrow."

"Yes. They must've been very stealthy."

"And after you gave chase, I bolted up and looked around, but I didn't see a soul. In fact, we haven't seen anyone else out here before or after."

"That's not entirely correct. We have seen one person." Hazel glanced back toward the house. "Fran."

CHAPTER TEN

Hazel admired Myrtle's demeanor as they walked back to the house. She was exceedingly jovial for someone who had just missed being skewered with an arrow. They agreed not to say anything about the incident to anyone except Gloria. She'd tried to downplay it to Fran but wasn't sure how much the girl would say about it. Unless the shooter *was* Fran, Hazel wasn't even sure if the shooter knew the arrow had missed the mark. Better to keep quiet and watch their behavior to see if anyone's expression or actions gave them away. That was, after all, her area of expertise.

But Hazel was disappointed to discover that everyone was in their rooms, resting up. Just as well. Hazel could use the opportunity to get some writing in. She wasn't about to leave Myrtle alone, though, so she brought her to Gloria's room and told her about the arrow incident. Gloria was upset, but Hazel cautioned her to tell no one. She left Myrtle in Gloria's capable and protective hands.

The fresh air must've been good for her, because she came up with a few more ideas for her book. She slipped into the kitchen and begged a morsel of fish to bring up to Dickens, who would undoubtedly be angry at being left alone for so long.

Alone in her room, Hazel gave Dickens the treat then sat at the desk and opened her notebook. She hadn't thought to bring her Remington portable typewriter because she usually spent the beginning of a novel jotting down notes in her notebook and scribbling a rough first draft. It wasn't until her ideas were all fleshed out that she set about typing out the story. She was making such good progress now, perhaps she should send for it. *Best not to get ahead of myself,* she thought as she selected the red Esterbrook pen and got down to the business of writing. If she kept going at this pace, she would be listening to the comforting clickety-clack of the typewriter keys in no time.

"*Meow.*" Dickens had jumped up onto the windowsill while Hazel had been absorbed in her writing. He rubbed his face against the wood frame then turned his pale eyes on Hazel, wrinkling his forehead slightly as he let out a pathetically soft meow.

"Yes, I know you want to go outside. Maybe later we could go in the garden," Hazel said. "Right now, I'm trying to finish my notes for this suspect."

"*Mereep.*" Dickens swatted her hand with his paw, causing her to blob ink on her perfectly formed sentence.

"Dickens, really! Must you?"

Dickens blinked innocently at her and twitched his velvety ears then rubbed his face against the windowpane.

"It *is* rather stuffy in here. I guess I could open the window and let some air in."

Hazel pushed the window up. A floral-scented breeze wafted in. And voices. Women's voices. She couldn't make out what they were saying, but…

She pushed her head out the window, craning to the right and left. Through the leaves of the oak tree next to her window, she could see Vera and Gloria standing by the garage. They were a study in opposites. Vera wore a sleek, sophisticated navy-blue dress that reached just below her knees. Gloria wore a brown-and-green summery frock with a lace edging and a cute cloche hat with a bouquet of yellow buttercups on the side. Were they arguing? Apparently, Wes wasn't the only one Vera argued with.

Snatches of harshly whispered words floated up.

"… leave … alone."

"Wouldn't want to find out…"

"…. worry, you'll get what you deserve."

Then Gloria got into a black open two-seater slammed the door, and drove off. Vera turned on her heel, and Hazel noticed she had the box camera in her hand. She stopped in front of a birch tree and leaned forward to inspect a leaf then held the camera at waist height, pointed it toward the leaf, and turned the switch to snap the photo. Maybe Vera was a budding photographer, or maybe she just wanted to get out of the house. Wes had mentioned something about her excursions, but she had also mentioned something about him wandering around the property. Hazel wondered if they had been referring to recent events. Maybe one of them had sneaked out that morning and that was what had started the argument in the first place. And if one of them had sneaked out… had it been to shoot the arrow?

But a bow lying in a path was not enough proof to move either of them up on the suspect list. Fran must have also been close by, because Hazel was only gone a few minutes, and Fran had been sitting with

Myrtle when she returned. And where was Edward this morning?

Near as she could tell, almost all of Myrtle's relatives had means, motive, and opportunity to do her in. But, as with her books, Hazel knew that in real investigations, one needed physical proof. She didn't have anything solid that could tie any of the family members to the incidents against Myrtle. She probably wouldn't be able to find a physical item that linked any of Myrtle's relatives with any of the attempts. More than likely, she'd have to work out which one of them could have been in place when each attempt was made. Or at least eliminate one of them by proving they couldn't have been there.

Whichever method she used to find out who was doing this, Hazel had a feeling she had better do it fast. This morning's incident had proven without a doubt that someone was trying to kill Myrtle, and she was afraid that next time, they might not miss.

CHAPTER ELEVEN

Hazel spent the next few hours absorbed in her work. She was so engrossed that when she surfaced from her writing, she was surprised that it was well past three o'clock. Myrtle's afternoon guests would be arriving for tea at any minute! She changed into an ankle-length lavender tea dress and rushed downstairs.

Guests were mingling in the sitting room and dining room, where the staff was setting out delicate china cups and saucers. The dining table itself had been laid with a white linen tablecloth and several three-tiered serving dishes loaded with finger sandwiches, scones, and other goodies. Gloria hovered at Myrtle's elbow as Myrtle introduced Hazel to the Corsairs, the Browns, and the Masters. Hazel already knew a few of the other couples there. But she wasn't interested in any of the new guests. She was interested in Myrtle's family. None of them were acting any stranger than usual, and no one seemed surprised that Myrtle was alive. But, of course, they'd already had time to cover their surprise before Hazel came down.

She didn't notice anyone avoiding any of the dishes, but she doubted the killer would have the gumption to poison any of the food at the tea... especially with so many guests milling about. Still, Hazel took note that Vera avoided the salmon pâté, and Wes, who for once seemed relatively sober, favored the scones over the sandwiches.

Thoughts of poison made Hazel wonder just exactly *what* poison someone would be feeding Myrtle. Gloria had mentioned natural poisons, but something niggled at Hazel's mind. Hadn't Vera mentioned something about needing a cat to take care of the rats in the cottage? And where there were rats, there could be rat poison. Hazel made a mental note to try to visit the cottage to look around.

During tea, Myrtle seemed unfazed by the morning's attempt at her life. Perhaps she'd already forgotten, or maybe her breeding was such that she played the gracious hostess no matter what was really going on in the back of her mind.

After tea was over, Myrtle leapt up from the table, clapping her hands together to get everyone's attention. "Everyone! We have lawn games set up outside, and there are still plenty of hours of sunshine left!"

Chairs scraped on the floor as everyone stood, some people grabbing one last biscuit or scone on their way out through the French doors, which stood open to reveal the stone patio and sweeping lawn below.

Gloria caught up with Hazel. Looping her arm through Hazel's, she leaned in and whispered, "Have you made any progress?"

Hazel shook her head. "But now is a good opportunity to see who can shoot an arrow."

"Of course! Someone with mediocre skills probably shot that arrow this morning. A novice wouldn't have come as close, and a good shooter wouldn't have missed," Gloria said. "I knew you would think of ways to get to the bottom of this. Most of the family is over there. Let's go and see what they can do."

They headed toward the area, skirting a rousing game of croquet, which Myrtle appeared to be winning. Down at the archery field, Mel and Sarah

Brown were apparently having a good-natured competition with Edward and Vera while Wes looked on.

"Don't you shoot?" Hazel asked Wes.

Wes held up his bandaged hand. "Not today." He seemed relatively sober today, no slurring of the words, and his eyes, though red rimmed, were not glassy and unfocused like they had been the day before. The gears in her brain started turning as she looked at his hand. If he couldn't shoot the arrow now, he certainly wouldn't have been able to shoot it at Myrtle this morning. But was his hand really as damaged as he was implying, or was this a clever cover-up?

"When did you hurt your hand?" Hazel said casually.

Wes squinted as if trying to recall. "Oh, about three weeks ago. I was on a fishing trip with the boys and fell on the pier."

"And it's not healed yet?" Hazel probably should've kept the question to herself, judging by the narrowing of Wes's eyes, but she couldn't stop it from popping out. Surely a simple fall wouldn't have injured him so much that it would take more than three weeks for his hand to heal?

Wes shrugged. "I suppose I'm a slow healer."

"Bulls-eye!" Vera's excited voice interrupted their conversation, and they turned to see an arrow quivering right smack in the red center of the target. Vera, dressed in a sky-blue mid-calf sheath, practically jumped up and down. She glanced back at Wes for approval, and he smiled and nodded. Had a look of affection actually passed between them? Perhaps they had made up after this morning's argument.

"Bravo!" Edward's accolades earned Vera a scathing look from Fran, who had come to stand beside Hazel. Was Fran jealous of her father praising someone else?

"That was a lucky shot," Fran said.

Vera held the bow and arrow out for her. "Would you like to try to best me?"

Fran's lips pressed together, her eyes narrowed. "I would, but it appears you're in the middle of the challenge here."

"Oh no," Mrs. Brown said. "We were just shooting for fun. Go ahead."

Fran's eyes dropped to the bow. "Sorry, I can't. They're waving to me over there at the badminton net. We have a small tournament going."

Edward smiled patiently at his daughter. "It's

okay, Fran. We know you have other things that you excel at that Vera doesn't do well."

Fran shrugged and headed toward the badminton area.

"Poor kid can't shoot for beans." Edward gestured toward the target where his brown-feathered arrows pierced the outer ring. One had missed the target entirely and stuck straight out of the ground. "Gets her lack of skill from me, I suppose."

"I'll take a shot." Gloria took the bow, expertly nocked an arrow, and pulled it back, focusing one squinted eye on the target before smoothly letting the arrow fly. It sailed through the air, hitting the bulls-eye right next to Vera's.

"Show-off." Vera put down her bow. "She always hits the mark. My arm is tired. Who wants to play croquet? Wes, even you can handle that, am I right?"

Wes threw his arm around her shoulder and laughed. "That, even I can do."

Everyone sauntered off toward the croquet area, but Hazel stayed back. If Wes and Vera were going to be occupied with croquet, now might be the perfect time to look around the cottage for rat poison. Hazel wasn't convinced rat poison was what was causing Myrtle's indigestion. Though she did seem a bit confused at times, she didn't have any other symptoms like hair loss, skin lesions, or white lines on her nails, and she wasn't terribly ill. Still, it wouldn't hurt to snoop around. She eyed the grounds, trying to pick out a path she could take without being seen.

"He's a pretty good shot, too." Gloria had appeared beside Hazel and was staring at Wes as the others walked toward the croquet setup.

"But his hand injury keeps him from shooting," Hazel said.

"Or from shooting *well*. I'm not convinced his hand is as damaged as he likes people to think. Wes has always been one to engender sympathy. When we were little kids, he used to milk every little injury," Gloria said. "And I did notice he can hold a glass of scotch pretty well with it."

Hazel thought back to Gloria's earlier comment about how the person who shot the arrow that morning must not have been a very good shot. Now that she'd seen Gloria shooting, she could verify the girl knew what she was talking about. But even though Wes was a good shooter, would his hand injury have hampered his ability and made him miss the shot? Was Vera a good shooter, or was her hit on the bull's-eye just luck? Fran and Edward weren't good at shooting, but Edward's shots had been so far off, Hazel doubted he could have gotten so close to Myrtle. Or maybe he'd shot like that on purpose.

"You're not standing here thinking about archery, are you? You look like you're deep in thought. Are you narrowing in on who has been doing these things to my aunt?"

"Sort of. Actually, I was thinking I would like to get a look at the cottage while Wes and Vera are otherwise occupied."

Gloria nodded. "And you don't want anyone to see you."

"That's right."

"I think I can help. It just so happens I know of a way to get to the cottage around the other side of the house and no one will see us."

Gloria led Hazel into the house then out through a side door in the kitchen. They scurried across a short patch of lawn and into the woods, though the scurrying was unnecessary since the mansion itself hid them from view of everyone who was gathered in the backyard.

"What are you looking for?" Gloria asked.

"Remember I told you this morning that I found the bow that we think was used to shoot at Myrtle at the beginning of the path to the cottage?"

Gloria nodded.

"When I followed the path, Wes and Vera were at the cottage. They were in an argument, so I didn't go close to the house. I wasn't sure if they'd been going at it for a while or one of them had just come in," Hazel said. "You mentioned that you thought Myrtle's indigestion indicated poison, and I remembered Vera said they had rats in the cottage."

Gloria made a face. "Rats? I never heard that."

"It's possible. The cottage is set far from the house, and there's a field behind it. Maybe Vera mistook field mice for rats. It's also possible that someone might use rat poison for more than just eliminating rats."

"Good point." Gloria stopped in her tracks, her panicked eyes darting back in the direction of the house. "Do you think Auntie will be okay back there without us watching over her?"

"Of course. No one would dare try anything with all those witnesses about." *Would they?*

Gloria turned back toward the cottage.

"I hear you introduced Wes and Vera. That you two are old friends," Hazel said.

Gloria looked at her sharply. "Well, I wouldn't say we're *friends*. I did introduce them. Vera and I ran in the same crowd once."

By the set of Gloria's jaw, Hazel knew she didn't

want to talk about her relationship with Vera. It probably dredged up bad memories of an unhappy time. Though Hazel was curious about why Gloria and Vera had argued, she could tell Gloria wouldn't be forthcoming. And besides, it likely had nothing to do with what was going on with Myrtle. She didn't want to mention the drugs, because Gloria could be a good source of information, and she didn't want to get on her bad side.

They continued a few more steps in silence, and then Gloria's face softened. "They really do love each other."

"They seemed affectionate back there at the archery field, but this morning, I heard them having an awful argument," Hazel said.

"What about? Money?" Gloria asked. But before Hazel could answer, she continued. "I know they bicker a lot sometimes, but they really do love each other. Wes told me he'd do anything to keep Vera happy."

"Does Vera have family money?" Hazel asked. "She seems to have expensive clothing."

"She might have a little. They live in the cottage for free, so they don't have many expenses. A little bit of money would go a long way."

They came to the end of the path, and Hazel

held Gloria back from darting out into the clearing toward the cottage. She wanted to be sure no one was there who could see them. She didn't want Vera or Wes to know she'd been snooping around. "Are there gardeners or other people who might see us?"

Gloria shook her head. "The garden staff is all tied up over at the house with the lawn games. We're all alone."

They crept up to the front door, a large, thick piece of rustic oak, and tried the knob.

It was locked.

"Oh, bother." Gloria peered in the window as if expecting to find a big carton of rat poison on the table.

Hazel stepped up to the large window beside her and looked in. Inside, the cottage was sparsely decorated. The furniture looked old but well cared for. Hazel was surprised: with Wes's drinking and Vera's strange attitude, she hadn't expected them to keep a neat house.

"We might be able to get in the back door," Gloria suggested.

Hazel followed her to the back of the cottage, where she was surprised again to find a small, neatly kept kitchen garden just outside the door. The garden Fran had planted. She recognized mint, basil, tomatoes still green on the vine, chives, cucumbers, peppers, and one section of weedy flowers that she recognized as herbs. "Is this the garden Fran planted?"

Gloria nodded. "Wes loves fresh herbs. I come in and weed it for him sometimes. Lord knows Vera wouldn't. He gives me some of the produce from it."

"Nothing like fresh herbs and vegetables."

Gloria tried the door, but it was also locked.

"I suppose they don't trust someone not to walk in," Gloria said.

"Or don't want someone to see what's in there," Hazel added.

Gloria pressed her lips together. "Seems dangerous to keep poison in the house."

Hazel followed her gaze as it came to rest on a small shed at the edge of the garden. She had a point: a shed was a much better place to keep poison.

The toolshed had a simple latch with no lock. The door creaked open, and Hazel peered into the darkness, the slice of sunlight filtering in from the doorway the only source of light. Even in the dim light, the box with the giant rat lying on its back, toes pointed in the air, was unmistakable.

"There it is!" Gloria pointed to the box.

But something else had captured Hazel's attention. Over in the corner, amidst a pile of rusty tools with worn, rotted handles, was a brand-new garden spade with a thin pointed blade that looked, from where Hazel was standing, to be quite sharp. The exact type of blade that would have been needed to sabotage the brick walkway.

CHAPTER TWELVE

Hazel chose to keep her thoughts on the spade to herself. Even though Gloria was on "her side," she'd learned long ago that it never paid to give up too much information. She'd already given her enough with the discovery of the rat poison, and while she felt reasonably comfortable that Gloria wasn't a blabbermouth, all it would take was for her to mention the rat poison or the spade to the wrong person, and the killer might try to escalate his or her plan.

By the time they got back to the gathering, the late-afternoon sun was casting long shadows of golden light on the ground. The guests were starting to gather their things and leave. The staff was disassembling the archery, badminton, and croquet equipment.

After the last guest had driven away, Myrtle turned to Hazel. "Are you hungry? We should have Cook put together a late dinner. We only had those tiny sandwiches at tea, and I've worked up an appetite with all this activity."

"Me too," Wes said.

"Yes, let's have Cook put something together." Vera linked her arm through Wes's, and they walked toward the front door.

Myrtle pulled Hazel to the side as the others walked into the house. "Have you found out anything?"

"Nothing conclusive. Don't worry… we won't let anything happen to you."

Myrtle gave her a funny look. "Are you sure this all couldn't just be coincidence? I mean, no one tried to harm me at all this afternoon, and I really can't imagine that one of my relatives is trying to hurt me."

"It hardly seems like an accident now that an arrow was pointed right at you."

"We don't know that it was pointed right at me. It could've gone astray," Myrtle suggested hopefully. "Have you seen how bad a shot some of my family are…"

Hazel patted her arm. "Maybe. Don't worry, I'll get to the bottom of it whatever is going on."

Myrtle's cook must've been anticipating the request, because a hot meal was ready as Hazel and Myrtle walked into the dining room. Hazel kept a close eye on who was eating what. She didn't think anyone would have had a chance to poison Myrtle's food, as they'd all been outside... unless they'd sneaked into the kitchen earlier that day. From what she could see, no one avoided any of the dishes. Even Vera seemed to fill her usually sparse plate. Wes had a good appetite, too, and Hazel noticed he washed it down with several glasses of whiskey, which he had no problem holding in his injured hand.

"I hope everyone had a good day today," Myrtle said. "I think the guests had fun."

"Oh, it was tons of fun," Vera said. "I think my archery practice is paying off." Vera turned to Fran. "Did you win the badminton game?"

"I did." Fran slid her eyes to Edward. "At least that's something I'm good at."

Edward looked contrite. "Now, Fran, I didn't mean anything by that remark. You're a fairly good shot with a bow and arrow."

"What about you, Hazel?" Myrtle asked. "I hope your afternoon was enjoyable."

"Indeed it was," Hazel said. And it had been, but probably not in the way Myrtle meant. Hazel had learned that the stone cottage had rat poison, and a spade that could have sabotaged the brick path. Not only that, but Vera was decent at archery, as was Wes, although Wes's injured hand might hamper his ability. But Gloria had suggested the shooter wasn't a crack shot like herself, so that made Wes all the more suspicious if his injury threw off his aim. Fran and Edward, on the other hand, were not that great at archery. Though Edward had just said Fran was a fairly good shot, she'd declined to shoot this afternoon, so Hazel had not seen for herself.

Her eyes slid to Fran, who was slathering butter onto a cracker. Fran had been there this morning when the arrow had been shot at Myrtle. Fran was studying to be a nurse and would know all kinds of things about medicines, not to mention natural medicines and herbs that might act as a poison. Myrtle had said that Fran had been here almost before the doctor the day she mixed up her medicines. Was that because Fran had got word about it quickly through her nursing associations, as she'd said, or had Fran actually been close to Lowry House because she had sneaked in and switched the medications in the first place? Maybe Fran had lied about seeing Gloria at Fanuel Square to give herself an alibi. Earlier today, Fran had had no trouble pulling out the embedded arrow, stating that her nursing job required a lot of strength. Whoever had sabotaged the brick path would've needed strength. And Fran herself said she was the one who planted Vera and Wes's garden. Was she the one who had put the new spade in the toolshed?

"It was a grand time," Gloria, who had been unusually quiet through the whole meal, chimed in.

Vera glanced at Gloria. "I didn't see you there the *whole* time."

Gloria narrowed her eyes, and Hazel saw a flicker of anger in them. She remembered the argument from earlier that morning. What was going on between Gloria and Vera? Did Gloria suspect Vera was the one trying to harm Myrtle? Did Vera have a motive that Gloria knew about but wasn't coming forward with? Or did their strained relationship have something to do with their past?

"I didn't realize you had been watching me the whole time," Gloria said.

Vera shrugged and played with the sparkly necklace around her throat. "I wasn't. I was just concerned something might have happened to you."

Gloria forced a smile. "Don't worry. I'm fine."

An awkward silence fell over the table, then Myrtle clapped her hands together. "Well, I'm glad everyone had a good time. I need to celebrate my eightieth in style." She turned to Hazel. "Tomorrow will be even more fun. You might want to spend the day resting up, as the party should be quite lively, and we'll have a small band and champagne toasts at midnight. I was born at midnight, you know."

"That sounds lovely. Will there be a lot of guests?" Hazel was mostly thinking of how hard it was going to be to keep track of Myrtle amidst a throng of guests. Would someone try to murder her at her own party? Today, there had been just enough guests that Myrtle wouldn't get lost in the shuffle, so Hazel had felt confident there would be no attempts. However, if there would be a large crowd tomorrow night, someone could easily lure Myrtle aside. Then there would be a whole household of suspects to muddy the waters.

"Oh, about fifty or so guests," Myrtle said.

"Including the Rothingtons, I hear." Vera raised a brow at Gloria, who frowned, her eyes narrowing at Vera.

"Now Vera, I know you aren't keen on them." Myrtle glanced at Vera then turned her full attention on Hazel. "But that's old news. I hope you brought some finery, because we'll be dressed to the nines."

Hazel glanced at Gloria and Vera in their modern

fashions. She hadn't thought much about keeping current with fashions since Charles's death. Could she wear the new fashions without looking ridiculously as if she were trying to pass for a younger woman? Then again, it worked marvelously for Myrtle. "I may need to make a trip into town."

Myrtle waved her hand in the air. "Consider my driver your driver. Giles will take you wherever you want to go. There is a lovely dress shop right in Bergamot Square."

Hazel furrowed her brow. "Bergamot Square? I don't think I'm familiar with that."

"Oh, it's in a lovely, well-to-do area. You must visit Squires while you are there. It's a fabulous antique shop, and there's a lovely place for tea there, too. Gloria can tell you where it is. I saw her there early this afternoon," Edward said.

Gloria straightened in her chair and swiveled her head to look at Edward. "I wasn't there."

Edward pursed his lips. "You weren't? I could've sworn I saw you coming out of the side street. Abbot Mews."

Gloria shook her head. "No, that wasn't me. I never go to that part of the town. I can't afford it, and besides, I haven't left the house all day."

"Giles knows where it is." Wes leaned forward as

if sharing a secret. "He drives Vera there. She gets her jewelry used at a little antique jeweler in the square. It's very reasonably priced."

Vera frowned at Wes. "*Shhhh*, don't tell my secrets."

Fran glared at Vera with disapproval, then her gaze flicked to Hazel. "I shan't go there. It's so *common* to buy used jewelry."

"Indeed," Gloria said. "You don't need jewelry anyway, do you, Hazel?"

Hazel looked down at her unadorned neck, bare wrists, and ringless ink-stained fingers. "No. I prefer a less cluttered look."

The conversation turned to the weather, the latest fashions, and last month's Wimbledon championships. Apparently, since attending them in London, Myrtle had been contemplating installing a tennis court at Lowry House. But Hazel was only half paying attention. She was busy observing and contemplating. She'd noticed no one was acting the least bit surprised that Myrtle hadn't been shot in the head with an arrow earlier that day, nor had anyone, including Fran, mentioned the incident. Though that in itself didn't prove anything. Fran could've bought their story that it was an accident, or if she was the one who had shot it, she certainly wouldn't want to bring it up at dinner.

There was another thing that was bothering her, too. Gloria had lied about not leaving the house all day. Hazel had seen her get in the two-seater that morning after her fight with Vera. She didn't know if Gloria had gone to Bergamot Square as Edward had said, but why would she lie about leaving the house? Did it have something to do with whatever was going on between her and Vera? She'd sensed something in Gloria's demeanor earlier that day when they'd been talking about Vera and Wes. It was almost as if she felt sorry for Wes. Perhaps she felt responsible for having saddled him with Vera. And, since she and Vera had known each other for a long time, maybe she knew something about Vera that the rest of them didn't. Was that something the fact that Vera was capable of committing murder?

Hazel had only heard overheard bits and pieces of their conversation out of the window, but she knew it had been confrontational. There was somewhat of a warning in the words. Something about leaving someone alone and someone getting what they deserved. Did Gloria suspect Vera was the one trying to harm Myrtle? Had she been warning her to leave Myrtle alone? But if she suspected, why wouldn't she have said something? It was clear that Gloria was trying to help them find the culprit, so if she had suspicions, she would certainly share them… unless, for some reason, they shed a bad light on Gloria herself.

Vera certainly had a motive. Wes would stand to inherit a lot of money upon Myrtle's passing. Vera liked expensive outfits and jewelry. Gloria had said she thought Vera had a little money and that a little bit of money could go a long way, but Hazel doubted it would go as far as Vera wanted it to.

CHAPTER THIRTEEN

H azel did not make much progress on her book that night. Her mind was too full of suspects in Myrtle's potential murder to think about the suspects in her book. She woke up the next morning, eager to get to Bergamot Square. And not only to find a new dress for the evening's festivities. She had a sneaking suspicion answers to some of her questions might be found there as well.

Breakfast was a casual affair, with food set out on the sideboard. Since Edward and Gloria were staying at Lowry House for the festivities, they were already in the dining room, picking at the food. Wes and Vera wandered in through the open French doors. Why bother with making food in the cottage when you could come and eat it at the manor house?

Vera's eyes scanned the table. "Is our dear Fran ill this morning?"

"No," Edward pushed eggs onto his toast. "She ate earlier. Already out and about."

Vera sighed. "I could never be an early bird."

She and Wes proceeded to fill their plates and take their places at the table.

"How are you this morning, Myrtle?" Hazel asked.

"Very well, thank you." Myrtle's plate included a light breakfast of scrambled eggs. Her tall glass was filled with the green juice of her health elixir. She was chipper as ever, and Hazel was glad to see the previous day's arrow incident hadn't dampened her spirits.

When they were finished eating, Myrtle pushed her plate away and turned to Hazel. "I spoke to Giles early this morning and he'll have the car ready for you in the garage any time you want to leave."

"Wonderful." Hazel patted her lips with the linen napkin and stood. "I'll see you all later tonight, then."

Vera pushed away from the table. Grabbing her camera from the sideboard, she strolled out beside Hazel. "Are you going into town for your dress?" she asked as they walked out of the dining room.

"Yes, as I don't really have anything suitable. I wouldn't want to look out of place," Hazel replied.

"I doubt you'd be the only one out of place." Vera's eyes drifted over Hazel's shoulder, and she turned to see Fran in her usual dowdy dress, standing in the front doorway, as if just coming in from outside. Hazel wondered what Fran would wear to the party that evening. Did she wear expensive gowns? No matter what she had for clothing, Hazel figured she'd be decked out in the family cameos, or at least the ones that she owned.

"Some of us are more… restrained in our choice of attire." Fran looked Vera up and down with disdain.

"I'm sure you'll both look—"

"*Meeeeowww!*"

A blur of brown-and-cream fur streaked down the stairs.

"Dickens!" Hazel lunged after the cat, who appeared to be making a beeline for the kitchen.

"*Meroooo!*"

Dickens dodged left, avoiding Hazel, who smashed against an Edwardian table, setting a crystal vase rocking. She managed to catch it just before it plunged to the floor. Vera lunged after the cat, practically falling to the floor as she grabbed for him with one hand, the camera in the other. She scooped up the cat, cradling him to her chest. "I've got him."

She held Dickens like a baby, stroking his silky fur. "Such a beautiful cat. I didn't realize he had the run of the house."

Hazel took Dickens from her arms. "He's not supposed to."

"You'd better make sure you keep him in your room. It's not safe for the cat out here with rat poison around the place," Fran said.

Vera stared at Fran. "Rat poison? Where did you see rat poison?"

Fran's eyes flashed. "I didn't *see* it. You said you have rats at your place, so I supposed there must be poison."

Vera made a face. "Of course I wouldn't have *poison*. Animals could get into it and die. I love nature and animals." She held up her camera. "In fact, I'm going out to take pictures of the birds right now." She nodded at Hazel then said, "Have a nice day in town." She then turned and strode off toward the front door.

"Yes, do have a good time in town," Fran said. "Madam Germain will find you the perfect outfit. That's where Vera goes. But don't dally. You'll want to be well rested for the festivities tonight."

Hazel clutched Dickens even closer as he wriggled to get away, and started upstairs, admonishing the cat as she walked to her room. "You know you're not supposed to be out of the room. How are you getting out anyway? I do hope there isn't some secret passage… those are always so convenient in my books. Cliché. Of course, if there were one, the murderer would surely use it."

Hazel scanned the panels in the hallway as she passed. But she knew there wasn't a secret passage, as she'd been to Lowry House many times over the years and even inspected her own room. This wasn't the first time Dickens had escaped from a room, and no secret passage was necessary. Dickens, like most cats, was sneaky and clever. He knew how to bide his time. To wait for the housemaid to come in to make the bed or clean, then creep over to the door as she opened it and slither out without her even noticing. He'd done it before, and Hazel had no doubt that was exactly how he was getting out this time. Her suspicions were confirmed when she entered her room to see fresh flowers in the vase. She deposited Dickens on the bed with a stern warning and headed out to the driveway.

Bergamot Square was a bustle of activity. There were hardly any horse-drawn carriages anymore, as they had been replaced with motorcars and now the double-decker buses in what seemed like the span of a few years. It was a relatively small square, not nearly as large or busy as Regent Street or Trafalgar Square, and Hazel would have been able to find Madame Germain's dress shop easily even if Giles didn't know exactly where it was. They chatted amicably on the journey out. Hazel knew Giles, as he was married to Duffy's sister's second cousin's cousin, and all the downstairs people seemed to stick together no matter how loose the relations. Hazel was never one to treat the household staff like second-class citizens, so she treated him as an equal, and when they pulled up in front of the shop, she gave him instructions to go off and enjoy himself then pick her up in two hours.

Inside the shop was the complete opposite of the street. Where it had been busy and loud outside, it was quiet and sedate inside. Round sofas in pink velvet dotted the shop. Crystal chandeliers reflected prisms of light on the ivory-colored walls. Racks of dresses in a rainbow of silk and taffeta lined the walls. On the far wall were several curtained dressing rooms. An elegant-looking woman that Hazel guessed to be in her midsixties came from the back. She practically oozed confidence and refinement.

"Are you looking for a dress?" she asked.

"Indeed I am. Though I'm not sure if any of the new fashions are suitable."

The woman stood back, looked her up and down, and clucked and nodded. "I believe I have something that will be just perfect."

Madame Germain had been correct. Hazel was astounded at how the bright-red dress complimented her coloring and gave her a sophisticated air. Not tawdry, as she would have thought the color might be. She looked classy and elegant, and Madame assured her the scarlet red was one of this season's most popular colors. She even persuaded her to spring for the matching red elbow-length gloves.

It only took twenty minutes to decide on the dress, so with her purchases in her pink-and-white-striped bag, Hazel figured now was a good time to try to answer one of the questions that had been taking up space in the back of her mind. She couldn't for the life of her figure out why Gloria had lied about coming to Bergamot Square the day before. Maybe if she poked around, she would find the answer. Edward had mentioned a certain street—Abbott Mews—and Hazel found it three streets away.

Abbott Mews was not as nice or populated as the main street. It was more like an alleyway, with shops much less well kept. Hazel didn't see much down there that would attract Gloria. In fact, it was rather seedy. Was Gloria consorting with her old crowd again? It didn't seem like she was, from what Hazel had seen at Myrtle's. But why had she lied?

Hazel strolled down the street, but when the crowd thinned to mostly shabbily dressed men and the motor traffic disappeared altogether, she turned and made her way back. It wasn't until the second to the last shop that she noticed the sign in the window. Help wanted. Standing back and peering up at the sign, she saw it was a secretarial agency. The kind of place that arranged temporary employment. Had Gloria been here looking for a job and was embarrassed for her relatives to find out? Judging by Fran's snobby attitude about Vera acquiring used jewelry, Hazel wouldn't blame Gloria if she wanted to keep her job search to herself. Myrtle had mentioned that Gloria had a little bit of family money, and if she'd gone through it all, she probably didn't need Vera, Wes, Edward, and Fran making her feel uncomfortable about it.

Satisfied that she'd found her answer, Hazel hurried back to the main street. A black-and-gold oval sign hanging from a grand brick building a few shops down caught her eye. Squires Antiques. Wasn't that the antiques shop Edward had suggested she visit? She strolled to the shop, pausing to look at the antiques in the display window. Colorful glass, oil paintings, silver tea services, delicate figurines, and other trinkets. Hazel had plenty of antiques of her own at Hastings Manor. Five generations of her ancestors had lived there, and not a one of them had ever thrown a thing out. The place was practically bursting with William and Mary this and Louis XIV that.

A jewelry display caught her eye. Perhaps she should get a necklace to go with her new gown. The current style was long strings of beads that fell below the waist. Jet beads would look lovely with the red dress. She squinted to see the price. The beads were quite expensive, and though Hazel had plenty of money, she couldn't see the sense in spending it on costume jewelry. Something niggled her thoughts. Not everyone paid high prices for new jewelry. Vera bought her jewelry at the antique jewelers where you could get pre-owned jewelry at a fraction of the cost.

Hadn't Fran said the shop was near here?

Hazel turned away from the antiques shop window to look at the signs for the other establishments. No antique jeweler. But that type of shop might not be on the main street. She peered down the side street, her eyes zeroing in on a royal-blue sign. Haskell Antique Jewelers.

She wasn't sure if she even wanted a necklace. She really wasn't the jewelry-wearing type, but the idea that she might be able to find out more about Vera and her finances had taken hold. Hazel had no idea what one paid for used jewelry. Perhaps Vera didn't need very much money to keep herself in the jewels and fashions she was so fond of. Hazel knew there were charity shops where one could buy used dresses as well.

Hazel opened the door tentatively, the bell sounding as she stepped in. A gray-haired woman who had been talking to the shop assistant—a bespectacled man in a dark suit glanced at her quickly. Hazel looked the other way. Maybe the customers of this shop didn't want to be seen. She busied herself with looking into the nearest jewelry case as the woman and assistant went back to inspecting the ruby-and-emerald necklace that dripped from the assistant's hand.

The room was dotted with waist-high black-velvet-lined cases. One could look down inside to see a variety of sparkling jewelry. The prices were quite reasonable. The cases held all types of jewelry, from genuine gemstones to ostentatious paste replicas, but there was one piece that made Hazel take a sharp breath.

A cameo with deeply carved cherubs and angels ringed by rubies.

Had Vera traded in the cameo to pay for the modern jewelry she favored?

"Can I help you?" Hazel jerked her attention from the cameo to the assistant, who was now standing on the other side of the display case. The other customer must have left while Hazel was busy staring at the cameo, and he was now focusing his full attention on her.

Hazel tapped her index finger lightly on the glass of the case above the cameo. "I was wondering who—"

"Oh dear, I hope there isn't going to be any trouble." The man wrung his hands together in angst.

"Trouble?"

"You're not with the other person who was in earlier?"

"Other person?"

"Someone was in here asking about the cameo. And if you are planning on asking the same questions, I'm going to tell you the same thing. We do not divulge our clientele. In this business, discretion is paramount."

Someone else had been asking about the cameo? Was that why Gloria had come here and lied about it? Did the cameo have something to do with the argument Hazel had witnessed between Vera and Gloria? Now Hazel wanted answers. But she knew from the assistant's agitated manner that she couldn't just come out and ask him point-blank. She would have to employ one of the techniques she often had her detective use in her books. She had to pretend like she knew more than the assistant did.

"Yes, of course. I hope they didn't cause too much of a problem," Hazel said.

"Well, I should say she did. Yelling and carrying on like that. Why, she scared two of our regular customers right out of the shop." The man's voice was shaky.

"I'm sorry she would act that way." Hazel leaned over the display case and lowered her voice, as if telling him a confidence. "We have to be very careful with her."

"Is she not well?" The man tapped his head.

Hazel nodded grimly. "Yes. Unfortunately, she goes off the deep end about family heirlooms. Has a right thing for cameos, she does."

"Yes. That's her. She spouted off horrible things. Demanded to know who had consigned the cameo.

Said it belonged to her. She made violent threats against the consigner. Of course, I didn't let on who it was."

"Of course not. It's too bad, because normally, she's such a lovely girl, and those green eyes and copper hair. So angelic. Hard for people to believe she could be so violent."

The man pulled a face. "Green eyes and copper hair? I don't think we're talking about the same woman. The one who came in here was not angelic in the least. And she had dark hair and dark eyes. A right sour little thing she was."

Fran? Of course, Fran was the one who had mentioned that Vera bought used jewelry. Had she followed Vera here and seen her selling the cameo, or just happened to find out later? And why cause such a ruckus? Fran didn't seem like the type to cause a commotion, but maybe she *was* a little unstable.

"Oh right, of course. How silly of me. Yes, she would be the one looking for these cameos. They are family heirlooms, but I'm sure a member of the family legitimately sold them to you." Hazel looked at the assistant out of the corner of her eye.

The man straightened. "But of course. We insist on provenance for valuable items."

"Of course," Hazel said. "Unfortunately, young

people these days don't appreciate old heirlooms and would rather have the money."

"Yes, indeed. This one was spitting mad about it, too. Ran out ranting about revenge and all kinds of nasty things." The assistant shuddered.

Hazel left the shop with her mind whirling. Fran had been here and was spitting mad about the cameo. Of course she would be, as she coveted the family jewelry and would be livid to discover that Vera had sold the cameo to buy modern jewelry.

But Hazel wasn't worried about Fran's anger toward Vera. A darker thought had crossed her mind. If Vera was selling off the family jewelry, she would eventually run out of items to sell. Maybe she already had and was now in need of a new influx of money. Money she could only get if Wes inherited it from Myrtle.

CHAPTER FOURTEEN

W hen Hazel got back to Lowry House, everyone was in their rooms, resting up... including Dickens. Hazel was glad to see the cat hadn't wandered out again. She took her dress out of the bag and hung in the wardrobe then stood back to survey it. Her stomach fluttered with nerves at the thought of wearing it amidst a large party later that night. She hadn't attended many parties since Charles's death and felt awkward about attending alone, especially in a dress of such noticeable color.

Now was a perfect time to work on her novel. She ran her fingers lovingly over the row of pens, selecting the red Esterbrook. She opened her notebook and settled in to write, but the words wouldn't come. She leaned back in her chair, nibbling on the end of the pen. Dickens sat on the bed, watching her intently, his tail swishing back and forth.

"I know. I know." Hazel sighed and leaned over the notebook again. "I need to get back to work. Hemlock may not be the way to go for the poison. Though we could hide it easily in the carrot jelly. But who *eats* carrot jelly? I wonder if there isn't something better I could use that would be found in a home garden."

Home garden. Wes and Vera had a garden. Fran had planted it for them—for Wes, actually, since she didn't seem overly fond of Vera. Hazel closed her eyes, trying to remember what grew in it. Basil, tomatoes, cucumbers. None of those were poisonous. But there had been some other weedy herbs at the back of the garden. She made a note in the margin of her notebook to figure out which herbs would cause indigestion *and* confusion. She knew some herbs could be fatal, especially in elderly people like Myrtle whose system couldn't handle as much as a younger person's. But why would Fran want to kill Myrtle? That didn't make very much sense. Fran inherited nothing directly. Myrtle had verified that everything would be split between Wes and Edward. But Edward might share some of his inheritance with Fran right away. She already had the cameo from her mother; maybe she hoped he would give her the rest of the cameos he might inherit. And maybe Fran wanted to make sure he inherited those before Vera got her hands on them and sold off more of them.

Vera had denied having the rat poison in the shed. Why would she do that unless she was using it for something she shouldn't be? But, then again, there was Wes. Maybe Vera never went in the shed and Wes put the poison there. Wes might have sold the cameo to get money for Vera. She did goad him about it that morning Hazel overheard them in the cottage. Hazel had a good memory for conversations, which came in handy for her writing. She scrunched up her eyes and thought back, remembering Wes's exact words. "*Don't I provide for you when you need it?*"

And hadn't Gloria said that Wes would do *anything* for Vera?

"*Meow!*" Dickens batted a little piece of dried grass around the room, pushing it under the chair and then peeking underneath and shooting his paw out to bat it to the other side of the room.

"That's right, I'm grasping at straws." Hazel stood. "And you need something better to play with."

She rummaged around in her luggage and pulled out a little felt mouse, which she skidded across the floor. Dickens pounced on it then skewered it with a sharp claw and threw it in the air.

When Dickens had his fill of playing, he hopped up on the bed and crawled on the pillow then curled up into a purring ball of fur.

"Good idea." Hazel lay on the bed beside him. She was making no progression on her book and needed to rest up for the party. She was going to need all her energy to keep her eye on Myrtle and ensure someone didn't plan to use the camouflage of a busy party to make another attempt.

CHAPTER FIFTEEN

Myrtle had arranged for the staff to deliver a light dinner to everyone's rooms. No sense in having a formal dinner when they would be stuffing themselves on the many appetizers and finger foods that would circulate the party. Hazel picked at her meal, tried to write some more in her book, and then finally, when she could put it off no longer, she changed into the red dress. The silky material fell around her body perfectly, so as to show off her curves in a subtle manner. She pushed away the bittersweet thought that Charles would've liked it.

She made sure Dickens had enough food and toys to keep him occupied. She didn't think the house-maid would be tending to her room during the party, but she didn't want to take any chances on him wandering out. There was no telling what kind of harm could come to him with a house full of party-goers and trays of canapés.

She hadn't bought any jewelry on her trip to town, but the dress looked good without it. Sophisticated. She clipped her mother's pearl-and-diamond earrings to her ears, pulled on her gloves, and made her way downstairs.

When Hazel reached the landing, she could see Vera standing at the bottom of the stairs in a silver gown, dripping with crystal—or was it diamond—jewelry. Beside her, Wes looked handsome in evening dress. Hazel hesitated on the landing, sensing an intimate moment between them as Vera reached up to straighten his bow-tie. Was it real affection, or was Vera more taken with his potential inheritance?

As Wes walked away, Fran, in a plain slate-gray dress unadorned with anything that might jazz it up, melted out of the shadows of the hallway and headed toward Vera. Closer now, Hazel could see she did in fact have some jewelry on—the ever-present cameo brooch and a matching bracelet.

"Don't you look lovely," Fran said sarcastically, eyeing Vera up and down.

"You don't have to say it like *that*. Just because you don't care to wear the latest fashions doesn't mean that you should take offense with the rest of us."

"You wouldn't even have these fashions if you didn't get them through sneaky means."

"Whatever you do mean?"

"I know what you did with the cameos."

Vera laughed. "Cameos? Those old things? She looked pointedly at Fran's neck. "But I see you like to wear them." She lifted the long, glittery strands of necklace that hung in layers on her chest, letting the beads drip through her fingers like crystal rain. "Just because I prefer to wear the modern styles is no reason to mock me. You see, the cameos just wouldn't go with my outfit."

Gloria sailed around the corner, looking sophisticated and charming in an emerald-green gown that set off her eyes. Unlike Vera's extra-sparkly accessories, she wore a simple necklace dotted with green stones. Her gown was lovely but looked to be off-the-rack, not custom-made like Vera's. She nodded at Fran and Vera then sailed off toward the kitchen.

Fran leaned toward Vera and hissed, barely loud enough for Hazel to overhear, "You'd better not sell off any more family valuables, or I'll make sure it's the last thing you do." And then she turned and stormed off, leaving Vera standing there alone.

From Hazel's vantage point, she could see Vera smirk, and even though she muttered the next words,

Hazel could decipher them by watching her scarlet lips. "That's what you think." Then she turned on her heel and headed toward the front parlor, where the band was tuning up.

Myrtle appeared in the hallway, her heels clicking on the marble flooring as Hazel descended the rest of the stairs. She wore a gown in several shades of blue accented in silver, an intricate diamond-and-pearl necklace, and jewel-studded silver gloves. Her freshly hennaed hair was vibrant.

"Why, don't you look lovely, my dear." She waved her hand up and down Hazel's body, her bejeweled gloves glittering rainbows in the light. "It's so nice to see you dressed up. You used to always dress so nicely with Charles."

Hazel paused momentarily at the pang of sadness that Charles's name evoked. Then she plastered a smile on her face. "You look divine, Myrtle. No one will believe you are eighty years old. Where did you get those gloves?"

"These things? I got them on my last trip to London. Gloria and I were both quite taken with them… but, honestly, they're very itchy." She scratched her wrist. "But one must make sacrifices for fashion." Myrtle hooked her arm through Hazel's.

"Now, come along into the sitting room. The first guests will be arriving any minute."

It wasn't even a minute before the arrivals started, and once they did, it was as if someone had turned on a tap. Hazel had all she could do to keep Myrtle in her sights, especially since there were many at the party who wanted to monopolize her attention. She'd forgotten how much she hated being thought of as a celebrity. But she accepted the compliments and praise for her novels as graciously as she could while trying to juggle tiny plates of hors d'oeuvres and keep one eye on Myrtle.

After a few dizzying hours, Hazel and Gloria worked out a system where they would give each other eye signals from across the room, signifying which one would keep their eye on Myrtle. That way each of them could at least enjoy part of the party.

Myrtle glided through the crowd, joking and sipping wine as if she hadn't a care in the world. She hadn't exhibited any of her forgetfulness or stomach upset since that first day, and Hazel wondered if the killer was holding off on the poison. Perhaps they had a more sinister plan now. Hazel, on the other hand, was wilting under the challenge of keeping track of the energetic Myrtle. She could barely keep up with the conversations she was having and wondered if people thought she had some sort of medical problem with the way her eyes were constantly darting around looking for Myrtle. At least it kept her from missing the presence of Charles at her side.

Everyone else seemed to be having a heck of a time. Fran was unusually social, and Hazel even saw her laugh once. Wes might have tipped the bottle a few too many times, but Vera was living it up—lively and animated and flirting with numerous handsome gentlemen. The three women seemed to have put their differences aside at one point, because Hazel saw Gloria snagging drinks off a tray and handing them to Vera and Fran as the three of them stood in a circle with Myrtle. Hazel wondered if the smiles on their faces were genuine, or they were just pretending for Myrtle's benefit.

By the time midnight rolled around, Hazel was exhausted.

"Everyone! Everyone!" Myrtle's voice rang through the house. It was Gloria's turn to keep an eye on her, but Hazel guessed from the sound that she was in the hall near the stairs, and Hazel turned in that direction. "It's almost time for the midnight champagne toast! Get your glasses ready."

Myrtle held her glass high in the air. The golden liquid in the glass sloshed around, a few drops spilling over onto her cameo ring. Myrtle wasn't very tall, so Hazel could barely see her hand wrapped around the stem of her glass as Myrtle made her way through the hall and toward the dining room, where there were even more partygoers filling their plates from the perpetual array of food set out on the buffets.

The crowd buzzed. The band played softly. Some people danced, but most preferred to mingle. The staff readied bottles of champagne and circulated trays with crystal champagne flutes.

Hazel felt a momentary panic. Where had Myrtle gone? Was it her turn to keep an eye on her? She scanned the crowd. Gloria was nowhere to be seen. Fran was chatting with a gentleman in the corner. Vera was draped over Wes as if she'd had too much to drink. Wes was leading her off toward the back hallway. At least if Vera were indisposed, Hazel wouldn't have to worry about *her* making an attempt on Myrtle. If she was, indeed, the one who had been making them.

Hazel thought she heard Myrtle's voice coming from the south end of the house and pushed her way through the crowd toward it, running into Gloria halfway.

"Have you seen Myrtle?" Hazel asked.

Gloria nodded, to Hazel's relief. "Yes. She's in the sitting room."

She turned to try to figure out the quickest way to the sitting room. When had the crowd got so thick?

"I'll head that way." Gloria nodded toward the door at one end of the room. "And you go the other way." She nodded at the hallway exit. "We'll see which one of us can elbow our way to her first."

The crowd had a happy, upbeat vibe, but trepidation bloomed in Hazel's chest as she made her way through it. The popping of corks filled the house, startling Hazel. They sounded just like gunshots.

She spilled into the hallway. Was Myrtle still speaking? She couldn't hear her anymore. She jostled a woman in a peacock-blue gown, who spilled some champagne on Hazel's dress. Hazel couldn't worry about that now. She rushed toward the sitting room, pushing in through the doorway.

Where was Myrtle?

She stood on tiptoe, scanning the crowd for Myrtle's sparkly gloves or Gloria's emerald gown. She didn't see either.

Pushing her way back out, she hurried toward the front parlor as more corks popped and partygoers cheered. Hadn't she just heard Myrtle's voice coming from that direction?

She couldn't hear anything anymore. There was a clamor of people drinking and clinking glasses. The band had got louder. Had Myrtle already made a toast? She'd been so focused on navigating the crowd, she hadn't even noticed.

She pushed into the sitting room. No Myrtle. Hazel's anxiety went into overdrive. Surely no one would try to kill her during a party with dozens of witnesses. Hazel was just being paranoid. She needed to relax. Gloria had probably found Myrtle anyway and was watching over her right now. It was unlikely anything would happen at the party.

And then a shrill scream pierced the air.

CHAPTER SIXTEEN

Hazel's heart lurched. The scream had come from her left. She whirled in that direction. The entire house had become silent for a split second and then erupted in chattering chaos while Hazel took off at a gallop.

The screaming had stopped, but Hazel had already homed in on its direction. The library. She rocketed down the main hall then turned toward the back hall, where the library was located. She skidded to a stop in front of the doorway. An older gray-haired woman in a blue taffeta gown was standing inside the room, facing the door. Her mouth was wide, her eyes huge as she stared at a chair whose back was facing Hazel.

Hazel's eyes dropped to the chair. The very one

she'd sat in the day she'd talked to Myrtle about the incidents that had been happening at Lowry House. But now someone else was in the chair. She could just see a wisp of henna-red hair peeking out from the side. One glittery bejeweled glove was draped on the table beside the chair. And the worst thing? A small black hole in the back of the chair. A bullet hole.

Myrtle? How could that be? She was supposed to be giving a toast. How had she ended up in a chair in the library?

Edward was coming up the hallway behind her. "Hazel, what is it?"

"Get the police," Hazel said to Edward, but her eyes remained glued to the chair. Her feet felt like lead. The gray-haired woman stared at her with large eyes. Edward hurried off at her request. Apparently, no one else had realized that this was where the scream had come from, since the hallway outside the room was empty.

Hazel's heart was heavy as she rounded the chair. She'd failed Myrtle.

She screwed her eyes shut, steeling herself for what she might see. She knew from Charles's cases that exit wounds could get pretty messy. She didn't want to see Myrtle in that condition, especially since it had been her job to protect her.

Hazel wasn't prepared for what she saw when she opened her eyes. Her breath caught in her throat, her lungs feeling as if they were devoid of air.

The victim wasn't Myrtle.

It was Vera.

A wave of partygoers appeared in the doorway, looks of concern on their faces. They tried to push into the room, but Hazel held up her palms to stop them. "Don't come any closer... please stay out of the room."

The woman glanced from the partygoers to Hazel and back to Vera. "Is she…"

"I'm afraid so." Hazel put her arm around the woman and led her to a chair, pushing her down into it. The woman was in shock.

Gloria appeared in the doorway, her eyes widening when she noticed the chair. Hazel imagined she was thinking the same exact thing that Hazel had thought. From that position in the doorway, the face of the chair's occupant could not be seen. All that was visible was the red hair and the gloves. She would assume it was Myrtle. So when Gloria's questioning eyes flicked to Hazel's, Hazel shook her head.

"What's going on here?" Fran stood in the doorway, her eyes flicking from Hazel to the hole in the chair.

"Everyone will have to get back into the hallway." Hazel left the woman in the chair, in search of some scotch or brandy. "I'm afraid this room is a murder scene."

A hush fell over the crowd, but Gloria ignored her plea to go back into the hall and ran to the front of the chair, her eyes widening. "Vera?"

She looked from Hazel back to the chair and then to Myrtle, who pushed her way through the people who still crowded the threshold. "What is going on?"

Gloria rushed over to Myrtle, putting a protective arm around her and ushering her out. "Auntie, something terrible has happened… Let's go and sit down."

The crowd made their way back to the other part of the house after Hazel once again instructed them to move along. She also instructed them not to leave until the police arrived. Then she turned her attention to the poor woman who had discovered Vera's body, and plied her with scotch. It seemed to revive her somewhat, but when she glanced back at the chair, she dissolved into tears.

Once the woman, Sadie Thompson, was sufficiently calm—or drunk—Hazel wasn't sure which, but judging by the way she'd sucked down the scotch, her bet was on the latter—she took the opportunity to go over the murder scene.

The gunshot had been to the back of the chair. The shooter must have mistaken Vera for Myrtle. They had the same exact hair color, and Hazel had seen that henna hair peeking out from the side of the chair and thought it was Myrtle herself. Had the killer seen that, too, along with the sparkly glove on the table, and assumed it was Myrtle? And what *was* Vera doing with Myrtle's gloves?

Hazel hadn't been far off in thinking the corks were gunshots. The killer had used that as cover.

"No! I don't believe it!" Wes's voice rang from the hallway. "Let me go! I must see her!"

He stumbled into the room, clearly drunk. His eyes were red, his face slack with shock. He looked like a wounded animal, darting his gaze from the chair to Hazel. "It's not Vera. It can't be."

But even as he came around to the front of the chair, Hazel could see it was sinking in. When he saw that it really was Vera, he sank down to his knees, weeping.

Hazel managed to get him onto a sofa and ply him with some of the scotch. At this rate, she'd owe Myrtle another bottle. It was an expensive brand, too. "I'm so sorry, Wes."

"She didn't even have that much to drink. But she wasn't feeling well. She wanted to rest a bit." He sniffed, rubbed his eyes, and looked at Hazel. "Who would have done this? Why would anyone want to kill Vera?"

CHAPTER SEVENTEEN

B y the time the police got there, Hazel was more than happy to get out of the room. Wes had been inconsolable. Luckily, a doctor was at the party and had given him something to calm his nerves. Myrtle, on the other hand, was as cool as a cucumber and had taken Wes to one of the bedrooms, tending to him like a mother hen. Perhaps mothering him kept her preoccupied and her thoughts away from the murder.

One police officer was stationed at the door, getting the names and vital information of the party-goers whom they were letting go home. The family members were probably their biggest suspects, as was common. At least that was how it always worked in Hazel's books. Hazel sat in a small, cozy sewing room just off the dining room with Gloria, watching the steam spiral out of their dainty chintz teacups.

"Should we tell them about the attempts on Auntie?" Gloria asked.

"I was wondering about that myself. We'd have to do that carefully so they don't just dismiss us out of hand. The police don't often like the public butting in," Hazel said.

"But don't you have friends? Connections with the police? You're well respected, and I heard they've even called you in on cases a few times. Surely whatever you say would carry a lot of weight."

Pride swelled in Hazel's chest. Charles had always listened to her theories and ideas about the various murder cases that he had discussed with her. And she had helped him solve a few. Even after he died, Scotland Yard had consulted with her here and there, but she didn't know if that was just out of respect for Charles's memory or if they actually valued her thoughts. Besides, the only one who seemed to want her advice was Detective Chief Inspector Gibson, and he wasn't on this case. Constable Lowell, a midforties, slightly balding, and rather serious man whom Hazel had never met before, was leading it.

Hazel was startled to realize that she actually wished Gibson were around. He would listen to her.

Oh, it wouldn't be like it had been with Charles. Nothing could ever be like that. But with Gibson's approval, she would certainly have a lot more leverage to contribute to the case. Though, admittedly, Hazel was stumped. Her main suspect had been Vera, but clearly, she must have been wrong about that. Unless…

"You don't suppose someone was really trying to kill *Vera* all this time, do you?" Hazel asked.

Gloria's brows shot up. "Vera? I know her personality was abrasive, but I don't think anyone would kill her. Besides, who would gain from it?"

"Good point. She didn't have any money." Hazel sipped her tea then looked at Gloria out of the corner of her eye. "But I did hear her and Wes argue. It could've been a crime of passion. And Fran seemed pretty angry with her earlier." Hazel didn't mention the conversation she'd overheard between Fran and Vera earlier, but she couldn't help but recall Fran's parting words "…*I'll make sure it's the last thing you do.*"

Gloria shook her head. "Vera and Wes did bicker and argue, but they were devoted to each other. Wes would never hurt her… though he does get in his moods. But he's never been violent before, just depressed. It had to be someone who mistook her for Auntie. The way she was in that chair when I came into the room, *I* thought it was Auntie myself. The gloves. The hair."

Hazel nodded. She'd thought the same thing. In her novels, she always suspected the spouse first, but she'd seen the true affection between Wes and Vera despite their differences, and Wes had appeared totally devastated. The gunshot had come through the back of the chair, meaning the killer never even saw the victim's face. Which made her wonder, had Wes been a little *too* devastated? The kind of devastation that combines grief *and* guilt. What if he had tried to kill Myrtle and had killed Vera by mistake? But wouldn't he have known it was Vera in the library? By his own account, he'd just situated her there… unless he was lying.

"It sure would be good to know what the police are thinking. Poor Auntie, I worry about her terribly," Gloria said.

"Well, this unfortunate incident might help flush out the killer sooner. Whoever killed Vera is the same person making the attempts on Myrtle. Once the police arrest them, Myrtle will be safe," Hazel said.

"If we tell them about all the things that have happened, and you compare clues with them, it might help speed things up," Gloria said hopefully.

"Maybe I can find a good opportunity to mention

the other incidents. We should go and see if we can find out anything that's going on." Hazel pushed up from her chair and turned just as a figure appeared in the door.

"Mrs. Martin. Why am I not surprised to see you here?"

"Detective Chief Inspector Gibson. How lovely to see you." Hazel tried to hide her surprise—and delight—from the tall man who stood in the doorway. His dark brow was furrowed in mock suspicion, but the twinkle in his brown eyes was welcoming. Was he happy to see her here? Hazel's heart gave a little twitch, and she wondered what it meant. Probably just excitement in knowing that if Gibson was on the case, she'd be able to insinuate herself into it.

Gibson's eyes dropped to Hazel's dress, and she felt her cheeks heat. He cleared his throat. "You look… good. I didn't realize you were friends with the Pembrokes."

Hazel nodded. "Yes. Old friends. You don't think I just randomly turn up at murders all the time, do you?"

"You do turn up at a lot of them," he said.

"And just what, exactly, are *you* doing here? Isn't Constable Lowell in charge?"

"I happened to be in the area, and they wanted to

put someone with a higher rank on the case. Well-known, prominent people like the Pembrokes command our utmost attention," Gibson said. "Speaking of which, perhaps we could have a little chat. I would like to get your ideas. I know you were one of the first on the scene, and your powers of observation are unparalleled."

Hazel blushed at the compliment. Maybe it wasn't such a bad thing that her staff seemed intent on setting her up with Gibson. He was rather charming, and his strong jaw, broad shoulders, and kind eyes did have a strange effect on her that was not altogether unpleasant. Not that she was looking for that sort of thing. It was too soon.

"I was just leaving. You can talk in here." Gloria shot Hazel a knowing look and left the room.

"Tea?" Hazel asked as she sat back down, eager to fill Gibson in on all her suspicions.

CHAPTER EIGHTEEN

Gibson listened attentively while Hazel described what she'd seen when she entered the library and found Vera. Unfortunately, she couldn't shed much light on the subject, because she hadn't seen much. She mentioned how, at first, she'd thought the victim was Myrtle, and then hesitantly told him about the attempts on Myrtle's life to date.

Gibson scribbled it all down in a small notebook, as if he truly did find her observations important. Hazel noticed with approval that he used a simple black Parker fountain pen. Reliable and practical. She was glad Gibson had shown up, as she doubted Constable Lowell would have given her suspicions the same attention.

"So you think Mrs. Pembroke—Vera Pembroke—was murdered by mistake?" Gibson asked.

Hazel nodded. "I believe she was mistaken for Myrtle. Their hair is the same color, and she had Myrtle's gloves on the table beside her. Unless Vera was the target and all the incidents I mentioned that happened to Myrtle were just coincidence."

Gibson pressed his lips together. "There seems to be a logical explanation for all of them. Or maybe someone was targeting Vera all along and Myrtle was on the receiving end by mistake."

Hazel's eyes narrowed. "That could be… No. Myrtle's pills were tampered with, and that would have nothing to do with Vera. Vera didn't walk the path, and Vera never sat in the rose garden. And I don't think they are coincidences, because when you add them all together, it seems a little too convenient for them all to happen in such a short period of time. I still say the intended victim was Myrtle."

"Okay, then who do you suspect is behind them?"

Hazel hesitated. She'd been leaning toward Vera as her main suspect. Now she had to rethink all of her clues. She didn't want to go giving information to Gibson when she didn't have it all sorted out in her head yet. "As near as I can tell, Myrtle has no enemies, so I assume greed is the motivation."

"Yes, it usually is for the money, isn't it?" Gibson said. "At least that's how it is in your novels."

Hazel blushed. "You've read my novels?"

"Every one of them." Gibson's kind brown eyes held hers for a few seconds.

Hazel looked away. "It's often the spouse, too. But Myrtle's is dead."

Gibson nodded and scribbled in the notebook again. "I suppose you already know who would inherit from her."

"Wes and Edward."

"And which one of them do you think could be the killer?"

"Well, to be honest, I'm not really sure. Edward does seem to covet the fine antiques Myrtle owns, and he would inherit a lot of them plus money, but Wes seems to need the money more than Edward." And then there was Fran and the cameos. No, that was reaching. It was more likely to be Wes or Edward.

"And you can tie both of them to these incidents?"

"I haven't found any exact proof that ties to either of them." Hazel thought about the rat poison and the spade in the toolshed of Wes's cottage. Anyone would be able to get into that shed, though. "But I haven't found any alibis that rule them out from doing any of the things either." Had she? Wes's broken hand would certainly have inhibited him from shooting the arrow, but could he still shoot? Was that why the arrow had missed? What about digging the walkway… had he broken his hand before or after Myrtle had fallen? The more she thought of it, the less likely Wes seemed to be the culprit. Maybe Hazel should've been looking at Edward a little harder.

"I'll keep all these things in mind—"

Constable Lowell appeared in the doorway. "We've got the names and addresses of all the guests. Sullivan has started interviewing the family." His eyes fell on Hazel. "And I hear Mrs. Martin is staying at the house. But it looks like you have taken care of interviewing her."

"Very good, Constable Lowell," Gibson said. "What about the woman who found the victim? Mrs. Thompson. Were you able to talk to her?"

"One of the guests is a doctor, and he looked her over. She's calmed down. Sent home with the rest. Says she went in to admire the books. She's quite a bibliophile. But we didn't learn anything from her. She didn't see anyone leaving the room."

"Has the murder weapon turned up?"

"Not exactly, but the coroner is here and had a look at the body. The bullet was a forty-four caliber. The gun was likely a small handgun, and apparently,

he have left something out that would be a clue? Would she even recognize it as such? Thankfully, Hazel was blessed with a good memory. If she kept her eyes open and took in as much as she could, maybe her subconscious would sift through the images and come up with something that was a true clue.

The bedroom was not as neat as the rest of the cottage. Colorful dresses lay thrown on the bed. Hazel felt a twinge of sadness, realizing Vera must have tried on several outfits for the party—the last party she would ever attend.

There were also photographs strewn on top of the dresser. A paper package of them lay on the windowsill. Vera's photographs that she'd taken with the box camera. Hazel picked up a stack and flipped through them quickly. They were actually quite good, all nature shots of trees and flowers. Even a frog. Guilt bloomed in Hazel's gut. She'd suspected Vera of trying to kill Myrtle, and she'd been wrong. The photographs were evidence that Vera was just a woman trying to enjoy life, not unlike Hazel herself. The fact wasn't lost on Hazel that if she had done a better job of figuring out who the killer was, Vera would be alive today.

The police went straight for the wardrobe, but

Hazel went straight for the old mahogany mirrored dressing table, the top of which was littered with jewelry. She could see most of it was costume, the long, sparkly necklaces that Vera favored. But a luxurious sterling silver jewelry box sat in the middle. Hazel glanced over her shoulder quickly to make sure that Lowell, Gibson, and the other constable who had joined them were occupied in the closet, then flipped open the top of the jewelry box.

Jewelry that could only be the real thing blinked up at her from inside the box. Rubies, emeralds, sapphires. A string of pearls snaked around glittery rings and earrings. There was lots of gold. A cameo brooch and earrings. A platinum ring with a giant pink stone. It was all in a messy pile. How much of it was in there, and what was at the bottom of the pile? She reached her index finger in to stir the bottom contents to the top. Her finger hit bottom quickly—

"Did you find a clue?" Hazel jumped. Gibson was standing right at her shoulder. When had he come over? But instead of being mad that she was touching things, his eyes danced with amusement.

Hazel turned and smiled at him. "I'm not sure if it's exactly a clue, but it looks like Vera had some expensive jewelry. Did you find the gun?"

She glanced over his shoulder to see that they'd

taken everything out of the closet. More clothes had been piled on the bed. Shoes lay out on the floor. A hatbox with its top off sat on top of the clothes.

"No gun," Gibson said.

Hazel's brows drew together. "That's odd. Why would Wes say he had a gun in here? He does drink a bit, though, so maybe he was mistaken."

"Or maybe he used it to kill his wife," Constable Lowell said. "Because if that gun was used in the murder at the house just a few hours ago, I don't think anyone would have had time to run back here and put it back."

CHAPTER NINETEEN

When Hazel returned to the house with the police, everyone was still up, anxiously awaiting the outcome of their search. Myrtle stressed the fact that the absence of the gun didn't mean a thing. She couldn't believe that Wes was the killer. She even pointed out that the house had been full of almost sixty guests. Any one of them could have shot Vera.

Hazel didn't have the heart to tell her that would be too much of a coincidence. Who else at the party would have wanted Vera dead? Everyone was exhausted, and retired shortly after the police left. Even Dickens seemed to sense something was going on, and he curled up next to Hazel on the bed and purred her to sleep. Surprisingly, she fell asleep quickly. Her last thoughts were of the gun. If Wes was the killer, why would he have sent them to the cottage to find it, knowing it wasn't there? Had he done that to get them out of the house to buy himself some time to hide it?

One thing was certain. The gun that killed Vera was likely still inside Lowry House.

The next morning, a bleary-eyed crew sat around the breakfast table.

"I can't believe Vera is gone." Myrtle wrung her hands, obviously distraught.

Gloria patted her shoulder. "Now, now, Auntie, it's very sad, but things could be worse."

Fran snorted. "I don't think Vera would agree."

"And to think those awful policemen suspect Wes!" Myrtle shook her head and then turned imploring eyes on Hazel. "Hazel, I do hope you'll stay on. I need your help in getting to the bottom of this

. I don't trust the police."

Though Hazel supposed most normal people would want to rush home rather than stay in a house where a murder had just occurred, with her, it was the opposite. She was driven to solve them. Not only that, but she'd already failed Myrtle once. If she'd been successful in discovering who had been attempting to harm Myrtle to begin with, Vera would not have been murdered. She could hardly leave now.

Hazel patted Myrtle's hand. "Of course I'll stay. Don't worry, we'll get to the bottom of this."

"And how is Wes holding up?" Gloria asked Myrtle. "I hope this doesn't push him off the deep end."

Myrtle straightened in her chair. "What do you mean? Wes is a sensitive boy, but he's not going to go off any deep end."

"He does get rather mopey," Edward said. Hazel studied him as he slathered butter on a scone. Where everyone else was red eyed and haggard looking, as if they hadn't had enough sleep, Edward seemed relatively unaffected by the recent events. But if he were the killer, wouldn't he be upset that he had killed Vera instead of Myrtle?

"I just don't understand how this happened." Myrtle sipped her green health elixir then let out a ladylike burp, covered her mouth, and shrugged. Hazel wondered if Myrtle was really this clueless. Didn't she realize the bullet had been meant for her? Hazel didn't want to enlighten her at the breakfast table in front of everyone. One of them could be the killer. And just what was the killer going to do now?

Would they make another attempt on Myrtle, or back off for a while until things settled down?

Hazel scanned the table. Fran was busy shoveling eggs onto a folded slice of toast. She didn't seem overly concerned about the previous night's murder. Edward sipped coffee, his eyes scanning the room. Was he taking inventory of the pieces he would eventually inherit?

Gloria's plate was still nearly full of her unfinished breakfast. She patted her lips with a napkin and turned to Myrtle. "I'll stay, too, if you want. You know… until the investigation is over."

"That would be nice, dear," Myrtle said.

"I can stay, too." Fran shot a dark look at Gloria and then smiled at Myrtle. "The family needs to be together at a time like this."

"I'd love to stay, too, but business calls, and I've got to get off to London for the afternoon tomorrow," Edward said. "I've an estate auction to attend."

His words immediately set Hazel on edge. Was he fleeing because he was the murderer? But whether he was here or not, if he was the killer, he would be discovered.

Finished with breakfast, they all left the table to go their separate ways. Gloria pulled Hazel and Myrtle into the small sewing room where Hazel had confessed her suspicions to Gibson the night before. The room still smelled faintly of his pine-scented cologne.

"I just don't understand." Myrtle looked at Gloria in confusion. "I thought you said someone was trying to harm *me*."

"They were." Gloria paced the room, agitated. "Whoever it was must have seen Vera in the chair and thought it was you."

Myrtle glanced at Hazel, her brow slightly furrowed. Hazel nodded. "You use the same hair dye, and she had your paste-jewelry gloves. How did she get those?"

Myrtle gasped. "Oh dear, I didn't think of that. The gloves were so itchy. I had to take them off. I tossed them on the table in the sitting room. Vera must have picked them up. Poor thing... she always was attracted to anything shiny."

"What about the police? Do they have any clues?" Gloria asked Hazel. "Would your detective friend tell you?"

"I don't know that he would," Hazel said. "But I can tell you they don't have any clues. Wes said there was a gun in his cottage, but we didn't find one."

"Are they sure the killer used Wes's gun?" Myrtle asked.

"No, but it was a similar model. Who else knew the gun was in the cottage?" Hazel asked.

Gloria shrugged. "I have no idea. Maybe Edward? I think I heard him and Wes talking about guns before."

"Maybe the gun wasn't even there. Wes's memory is a bit impaired from all the drinking he does. Did you see it when you cleaned for them that day they went to see Dr. Forrester in London about Wes's hand?" Myrtle asked Gloria.

Gloria shook her head. "No, but I wasn't snooping in their things, just cleaning. I imagine he would have kept it hidden away."

"Oh, this is all so disturbing," Myrtle said. "I mean, honestly, one of my own flesh and blood trying to kill *me* and then killing Vera instead…"

Hazel studied Myrtle. When she'd arrived at Lowry House, Myrtle had acted as if she were confused, but then over the course of Hazel's stay, she had seemed more lucid. This morning, though, she seemed confused again. Probably the stress of having someone murdered in her own home.

Gloria must have noticed Myrtle's confused state as well, and she pulled her out of the chair, putting her arm around her and leading her out of the room. "Why don't you get some rest? It was a late and disturbing night last night, and you're out of sorts."

"Good idea. I'll just be in my room. No, dear, you don't need to take me up there. I can find it myself."

Myrtle opened the door, and Fran appeared out of nowhere. "I'll take you, Grandma." She darted another look at Gloria, and this time her eyes held a sheen of triumph. Was Fran jealous of Gloria and Myrtle's relationship?

Gloria watched them walk away with a look of concern on her face. She closed the door and then lowered her voice. "Should we let Fran take Auntie to her room? What if Fran is the killer?"

"I just don't know what to think," Hazel said. "Fran doesn't seem to have much of a motive to kill your aunt. But I did notice there was no love lost between Fran and Vera."

Gloria snorted. "You can say that again. It's all so confusing."

"Indeed. But we have one fewer suspect now. I just wish I knew where everyone was at the time of Vera's murder, but the house was so crowded, and I was keeping my eye on Myrtle."

"Vera must have been shot when the champagne corks were popping off," Gloria said.

Hazel screwed her eyes shut and tried to recall the

events of the previous evening, but she couldn't remember seeing any of the family members during the time of the uncorking. She'd lost sight of Myrtle then run into Gloria, and the two of them had been focused on finding Myrtle while the champagne bottles were being opened. "Do you remember seeing any of the family members when the champagne was being uncorked?"

"No. I was busy looking for Auntie, remember?" Gloria narrowed her eyes. "I did see Wes and Vera shortly before running into you. They both seemed drunk, Vera especially. He was taking her somewhere to rest. I guess he must have taken her to the library."

Hazel felt a niggle of excitement, as if she were homing in on the killer. She knew better than to make a hasty accusation, but things weren't looking good for Wes. He had motive to want Myrtle dead. He had the same kind of gun that had killed Vera, and apparently, he was the last one to have seen the victim alive. But if he knew Vera was the one in the library and not Myrtle, then why would he have shot her?

CHAPTER TWENTY

An hour later, Mrs. Naughton tapped on the door, summoning Hazel. It appeared Gibson was there and wanted to consult with her. Hazel was flattered. She smoothed her dress and hurried downstairs.

Gibson was standing in the hall, cleanly shaven and in a tailored suit. How had she never noticed before how tall he was? Hazel was taller than most women, but Gibson practically towered over her. For a minute, she forgot he had summoned her to consult on police work.

"Detective Chief Inspector Gibson." Hazel nodded.

Gibson cleared his throat. "You can call me Michael."

Could she? She preferred to think of him as Gibson, and calling him Michael seemed rather informal. Gibson was safer. After all, she hardly knew him, but if it helped her get an "in" with the investigation… "What can I help you with… Michael?"

"I was wondering if we might walk the brick path you mentioned the other night…" He let his voice trail off and looked about as if to make sure no one could overhear. Naturally, he wouldn't want Hazel's suspicions to be known to everyone in the house. She appreciated that, and the fact that he actually thought her suspicions were something to consider.

"Certainly. It's a lovely day for a walk." Hazel led him out of the house and onto the brick pathway.

Once they were far from the house, he said, "Now, these other incidents, would Wes have been around at the time they happened?"

"He would have. He lives in the stone cottage, so he has access to the property. Unlike the others, he can come and go virtually undetected because he lives here."

"But the others were here the day the arrow was shot, right?"

"Yes. And there's another thing. I think some of them may have been lying about where they were at other times. It's possible any one of them could've sneaked into the house and changed her pills. And the indigestion… well, I talked to Wes this morning, and he grows Saint John's wort in his garden."

"Oh?" Gibson frowned at her, and Hazel realized he probably wasn't familiar with the side effects of Saint John's wort.

"It can cause confusion and stomach upset, among other things. It can also help elevate mood, which is what Wes says he uses it for."

"And now you think someone might've been feeding her the Saint John's wort and not rat poison?" Gibson asked.

"Perhaps."

"Saint John's wort could kill her?"

"No, but perhaps the killer thought it might. We may not be dealing with the savviest of killers here."

"Indeed," Gibson said.

They had come to the area that had been tampered with, and Hazel pointed to the exact spot and told him how she suspected someone had dug out the dirt underneath to make the bricks unstable. Gibson looked at it thoughtfully, even getting on his hands and knees to poke at the dirt and pry up a few bricks. Finally, he stood and brushed his large hands together, the dirt falling onto the ground. "It sure seems like someone could've tampered with it. But as with the St. Joseph's Ward—"

"Saint John's wort," Hazel interrupted.

"Right. Wort. Anyway, neither of those was guaranteed to kill. As you said, the killer is not very savvy."

They turned and started back toward the house. "That's what I thought, too, but a fall could really harm an old person like Myrtle. Just one small knock on the head, and she'd be a goner. And I suppose I could be wrong about the Saint John's wort. There was rat poison in the shed as well. Not to mention that the killer is an amateur and perhaps not thinking things through properly." Thoughts of Fran came to mind. She did seem to be impulsive when she got angry, and a little volatile. Prone to lashing out in the moment without thinking.

"The arrow would have been likely to kill Myrtle if it had found its mark."

"And the medicines. Even though she didn't take enough to do her real harm, whoever switched them might not have realized how many pills she would normally take."

"All of this has merit. But what I'd really like to see is some physical proof."

"Unfortunately, that is something I do not have." Hazel thought for a few seconds. "There is one thing, though; in my books, I often rule out suspects by proving they *couldn't* have done it. Wes has a broken hand. He showed me this morning that he cannot clench his fist, and so can't shoot a gun with his right hand."

"He could be faking that," Gibson pointed out.

"I thought of that. I know you have the chair for evidence… would you be able to tell if the gunshot was done from a right-handed or left-handed shooter?"

Gibson cocked his head to the side as if picturing the chair. He bent sideways as if tracing the bullet's trajectory through the chair in his mind. "The bullet was angled from east to west, which would indicate a right-handed shooter."

"Then, unless Wes is faking, perhaps we can rule him out."

"Perhaps. But you are making a lot of assumptions, Mrs. Martin."

"Hazel." Why had she asked him to call her that? She wasn't sure she wanted to be on such familiar terms with the inspector.

"What?"

"You can call me Hazel."

"Oh. Right. Good, then. Anyway, in the business of investigation, assumptions can be very dangerous. For example, the spade in the toolshed of the cottage may not have been the one used on the path."

"Well, I just…"

"Oh, I know. It *could* be the one that was used. But a garden as big and well cared for as this"— Gibson gestured toward the lavish gardens before them—"would surely have a variety of tools right in the main garage."

Hazel glanced toward the garage. It had once been just a big barn, with a second story where the groomsmen stayed. Part of it had been converted into a garage for motorcars. Darn it, Gibson had a point. Why hadn't she considered that? Of course there would be all kinds of tools that one could dig up a path with right in the garage. And anyone would have access to them. "You do have a point."

"You have good instincts, Hazel. But it never pays to make assumptions. The real clues can only be revealed by the logical systematic deduction of each specific piece of evidence, and in that way—"

"Of course!" Hazel interrupted him. Rude as it might be, she couldn't help herself. She had just realized what was wrong with her book. She'd made assumptions, and that was why her detective couldn't work out who the real killer was. "I'm very sorry, Michael. I don't mean to be rude, but I've just realized what is wrong with my book."

Hazel turned and ran up the path, leaving Gibson staring after her with an amused look on his face.

CHAPTER TWENTY-ONE

H azel had told Duffy to pick her up on Monday, so she found Giles in the garage and gave him a note instructing Duffy to hold off until further notice. She knew her household would be buzzing with excitement that she was "on a case." She smiled, picturing Maggie and Alice practically bursting for details. They would have to wait, though. It would be embarrassing to admit to them she was still a bit muddled about the whole case. She handed the note to Giles, who assured her it would make its way to Duffy quickly through their various relations, and then retired to her room. Dickens showed his delight in her return by weaving himself around her ankles until she tripped and almost fell to the floor.

"Alright, Dickens. We'll have a little bit of petting time." Hazel sat at the desk, and Dickens immediately jumped into her lap, nudging her hand with his head. She absently stroked his silky fur as she thought of the clues she had thus far.

Wes had brought up a good point about Vera's shady past, but it didn't seem likely that someone from her past would have been making attempts on Myrtle. Could Vera's murder be a big coincidence? Maybe someone from her past really had killed her and it had nothing to do with the attempts on Myrtle.

But the only ones at the party were the Rothingtons. It couldn't have been them—they were rich and powerful. They wouldn't stoop to murder, though it might not be a bad idea to find out *why* they didn't like Vera.

But Hazel had a feeling, and her feelings were usually right. It was an instinct that she used both in her books and in the cases she'd helped Charles with in real life. She was almost positive that Vera's killer was the same person who had tried to kill Myrtle; therefore, it was either Edward, Wes, or Fran. Unless it was one of the staff? Hazel almost laughed out loud at the thought. Unlike in her books, in real life, it was never usually the butler who had "done it."

"Let's look at the clues chronologically," Hazel said out loud.

Dickens purred and pushed his head harder

against her hand.

"The first incident was the brick pathway. Now, we've already determined that Fran, Edward, or Wes could have done that. Wes's hand was not injured at the time, and he has the spade in his toolshed."

"*Meow.*"

"Speaking of the toolshed, the rat poison was found in there, too. So he must have known about that. But Fran planted the garden, so she would have also known what was in the shed."

"*Mereww,*" Dickens agreed.

The garden reminded Hazel of the Saint John's wort. Wes had mentioned that it was in his garden. He was even drinking a tea made from it. Excited that she might be on to something, she turned in her chair to grab her notebook, dislodging Dickens, who thudded onto the floor with an angry meow.

Ignoring the cat, she pulled out her notebook and thumbed through it. "Let's see... chamomile, gumwort, mugweed. Oh yes, here it is—Saint John's wort." She ran down the list of symptoms she'd written for the herb with her ink-stained index finger, her heart beating faster when she noticed confusion and stomach upset were both on that list.

She turned back to Dickens, who was now rubbing his face against the leg of the desk. "What if it wasn't rat poison at all? What if someone was feeding Myrtle Saint John's wort?"

Dickens sat and blinked at her.

"You have a point. Why would someone feed her Saint John's wort?" Hazel consulted her notebook again. "They couldn't possibly feed her enough to kill her."

Dickens swished his tail back and forth.

"Right. Let's get on with the clues, then. So anyone could have dug up the path. But what about mixing up her pills?"

Dickens hopped up onto the bed and curled up in a ball, apparently already bored with the conversation about the clues.

Hazel continued on undaunted. "Fran is studying to be a nurse and knows about medicines. She would know exactly how many to mix in there. Wes admitted earlier that he frequently came into the house without anyone knowing he was here. Could he have sneaked in that night and switched the pills?"

Dickens stared at her unblinking from his spot on the bed.

"Or did Edward change them? Where was Edward that night? Where was he when the path was tampered with? And where was he when the arrow was shot?"

Dickens slit his eyes as if to say, "Yes, where *was* he?"

"For that matter, where were any of them? The bow was found on the path to the cottage, but anyone could've tossed it there. Fran was sitting with Myrtle when I returned from the cottage. And Fran must have lied about seeing Gloria at Fanuel Square the day Myrtle mixed up her pills, because Gloria was on holiday at Gull Landing. Fran was strong enough to dig up the path, and Fran planted the garden... so she would've known what was in the toolshed, including the rat poison... not to mention the Saint John's wort in the garden itself. Yet she'd specifically said she didn't *see* any poison when Vera asked her the morning Hazel went shopping. Had she lied twice?"

Hazel got up from the desk and walked the length of the room. "Fran also said she took care of Wes. She brought food. Did she have access to the house? And, if so, to the gun?"

Hazel paced around the room, the clues whirling in her mind. It seemed as if she couldn't rule any one of them out. But even though Fran looked like she could be guilty, she didn't have a motive. Edward didn't seem as suspicious as the others, though something about him niggled at the back of her mind... hadn't he been the first person besides her to get to the library last night after she'd heard Mrs. Thompson scream? And he hadn't seemed very upset about Vera this morning at breakfast, though admittedly he probably wasn't that close to her with Vera being his nephew's wife.

She paced back over to the desk and flopped in the chair. This was as frustrating as her book. She opened the notebook and flipped to the spot where she'd left off. Chapter twenty-seven, where the detective was just trying to add up all the clues and narrow down the list of suspects to the real killer. Just like in the case here at Lowry House, the detective in her book was stuck.

A dull fear worked its way into her heart. What if her earlier triumph of being able to write the book without Charles's input had been a premature victory? No. She'd come this far on her own. She was almost done, and she could do this on her own.

Too bad the suspects and the clues simply weren't adding up. Usually that meant she'd overlooked at least one key clue. She flipped back through her notebook, trying to find it. All the while, the little voice in the back of her head was wondering if she was also overlooking a key clue here in the mystery of the killer at Lowry House.

CHAPTER TWENTY-TWO

Hazel was deep into unraveling the plot of her book, looking for that one key clue, when a soft tap sounded at her door. She stood and attempted to pat down her hair, which stuck out in various directions from her running her fingers through it while trying to work her way through the maze of suspects and clues.

"Hazel, are you in there?" Gloria whispered from the other side of the door.

Hazel opened it and ushered Gloria in. She looked nervous.

"The police have been here talking to Wes, and now they want to know where everyone was last night at the time Vera was killed," Gloria said.

"What time was she killed?" Hazel asked.

"They say it was between midnight and one a.m."

"Well, we knew that. We could narrow down the time even closer than that, as a matter of fact. But we were all here at the party... surely the police are aware of that."

"They are. They want to know if any of us can corroborate where the others were exactly."

Hazel made a face. It sounded like Constable Lowell was grasping at straws. "You and I ran into each other quite a bit, and I saw you with Vera, Fran, and Myrtle, but that was earlier in the evening. I don't really see how any of this is going to help. There was a house full of people."

"Yes, and I doubt anyone was looking at their watch. They were busy drinking champagne," Gloria said.

"At least this does confirm one of my suspicions. Vera was shot when the champagne corks were popping. That's why no one heard the gunshot."

"Yes, I tried to tell Constable Lowell that. He's asking specifically if any of us saw Wes at that time, and I know he's looking at him as the prime suspect. I hate to say it, but..."

"You think Wes has been behind all of these attempts on Myrtle?" Hazel asked.

"I hate to think it," Gloria said. "Someone has

been doing this, and Wes had a lot to gain. Plus, he's been unstable since his mother died."

"But what about his hand? Would it have been possible for him to shoot the arrow or fire the gun?" Hazel asked.

"I don't think his hand is *that* bad. When we were children, he always made his injuries seem more severe. He wanted the attention. And besides, he babies his hands because he's a pianist." Gloria sighed. "Have you ever tried to do something you're really good at when you had an injury? You can still do it, but not as well. He could've shot the arrow, and the reason he missed is that his aim was off due to his hand. You did find the bow on the way to his cottage, am I right?" Gloria's eyes misted over. She was close to tears. The poor girl really must have affection for Wes. Hazel felt a flash of sympathy for Gloria. This whole thing must be terribly hard on her. Here she was, trying to save Myrtle, but in doing so, she had to condemn one of her other relatives.

But still, Hazel was not one hundred percent convinced of Wes's guilt, and if she couldn't write the ending of a novel unless she was one hundred percent convinced of her character's guilt, then she certainly couldn't do it in real life.

"I know this must be hard, Gloria, but we have to

find the right person. And I'm not convinced it's Wes."

Gloria's eyes widened. "You don't think it could be Fran or Edward, do you? I can't place Edward at any of the other attempts, and Fran has nothing to gain. There's no one else."

"You said Wes was a little unstable. Is that something that runs in the family?"

"It does. You mean Fran? Yes, she is a little odd. And unstable too." Gloria frowned. "You mean she might've been trying to kill Auntie even though she inherits nothing… because she's unstable?"

Hazel shrugged. "Perhaps. I just know that things may not be as we think they are."

"But all the clues seem to point straight to Wes. In fact, I think I saw Fran talking to some young man in the corner all night."

"Even when the corks were popping?" Hazel asked.

Gloria chewed her bottom lip. "I think so."

"You were pretty busy looking for Myrtle. Remember neither of us could find her?"

Gloria nodded. "That's right."

"So I don't think you could have had your eye on Fran, could you?"

"I don't know what to think anymore. I was

hoping to figure out who was doing this before anyone got killed. That way we could help Wes...or whomever...before they committed a drastic crime. But now it's too late. And if it is Cousin Wes, I doubt he would survive in prison. This is all so terrible." Gloria walked to the door. Her right hand on the knob, she turned back to Hazel. "I hope your doubts about Wes turn out to be true, but I'm not as optimistic. And if I'm right, he's going to need my support more than ever. I was just on my way to his room to see if I can get anything from the cottage for him. If you work anything out or hear anything from the police, will you let me know?"

"Of course."

Gloria left. Hazel sat at the writing desk, chewing lightly on the cap of the Sheaffer pen. Just like in her novel, here at Lowry House, something didn't add up.

CHAPTER TWENTY-THREE

Hazel wrote fast and furiously, using the Waterman pen Charles had given to her. Reality faded away as she drifted into the world of her characters. Working out who killed Vera was important, but finishing her book was important, too, and besides, the police were on the case now, so capturing the killer wasn't on her shoulders. She forgot all about Myrtle, Wes, and even Dickens, who lay on the chair in front of the fireplace. Her discussion with Gibson outside had made her realize that her detective had made a lot of assumptions. Because of those assumptions, he had not followed up properly and logically. It stung for her to admit it, but Gibson was right: she'd made big mistakes. But now she thought she knew how to correct them. Maybe she could get this book written without Charles after all.

After a while, Dickens must've become bored, because she heard him meowing and was vaguely aware of him butting up against her leg for attention. But she couldn't stop. She was on a roll, and as any novelist knew, one had to continue writing when they were in the fever of plot discovery. With any luck, she'd be able to finish her first draft by the time she left Lowry House, so she could start the second draft on her Remington when she got home.

Now, where was she? Oh yes, her detective was just about to follow up on some of the clues he'd neglected to follow up on because of the assumptions he'd made.

"*Meoooow.*"

Dickens's cry pulled her from her thoughts. But wait, hadn't she made the same mistake as her fictional detective? She had neglected to follow through on some clues because she'd assumed they were unimportant.

She'd neglected to follow up on her suspicions that Fran had lied about being in town the night Myrtle's pills were switched. And not only Fran; it was possible Edward had lied about seeing Gloria in Bergamot Square. Now why would he have done that? Was it possible either Fran or Edward was trying to set someone up? Maybe they were even working together to get rid of Myrtle.

Dickens rubbed against Hazel's ankle and purred loudly.

"Yes, I do think some extra checking is in order. The whereabouts of every family member must be checked. And the cameo I saw in the antique jewelers…."

Something niggled in the back of Hazel's mind. When she'd been in the cottage with the police, she'd notice some odd things about Vera's jewelry box, and now she realized one of those was that she'd seen a cameo in there. It had matched the Pembroke family cameos. If Vera had sold hers at the antique jeweler, then how could it be in her jewelry box?

Unfortunately, Hazel didn't have the clout to force the antique jeweler to reveal his client or to follow up on the whereabouts of the other family members. But, luckily, she knew someone who did.

She scribbled a note on the lavender notepaper and set out to find Detective Chief Inspector Gibson. With any luck, he would still be in the house, questioning people. She found him exiting the sitting room, where he had been interviewing Wes, a minute later.

"I was looking for you," Hazel said.

"Oh, really? That's funny, because the way you wandered off earlier made me think you didn't give my company a second thought. I'm glad you've decided otherwise."

Hazel blushed. "No, it's not that. It's this." She shoved the note into his hand and lowered her voice, leaning close to him. The pine scent of his cologne distracted her, and the twinkle in his eyes caused her tongue to tie up for a few seconds before she could say, "I need you to check out these alibis. What you said before was true. I had made some assumptions. And now I realize I didn't check things thoroughly, but I don't have the authority. But people have to answer questions asked by the police, so maybe you can send one of the constables to pursue these leads."

Gibson unfolded the note, a smile playing across his lips as he read it.

"Can you look into these, Gibson … err… I mean, Michael?" Hazel asked.

"Yes, I can. Hazel. In fact, I already have my best man on it."

Hazel's brows tugged together. "You do? But how could you—"

"Hazel. *Psst…*" Myrtle hovered in the doorway of the sitting room, gesturing for Hazel to join her.

"Oh, Myrtle… I was just—"

"Oh, no problem. Mrs. Martin and I were finished." Gibson smiled down at Hazel as he stuffed the paper into his top pocket then patted it with his fingertips. "And I have to continue on with my investigation now."

Myrtle pulled Hazel into the sitting room and closed the pocket door. She lowered her voice. "What's going on? Have they worked out who killed Vera?"

"Not yet. They're still looking into it." Hazel's eyes fell on the writing desk over by the window where gardenia-design notepaper was scattered across the desk. Two writing pens sat next to it. Not elegant, expensive pens as she'd imagined Myrtle would use. These were newer, cheap models. "Are you writing letters?"

Myrtle glanced over, her face twisting. "I must apologize to my guests for last night. I mean, how will I show my face in public? Can you imagine going to a party and ending up at a murder?"

"It certainly did put a damper on things." Hazel crossed to the desk, fingering the vase of colorful yellow buttercups.

"Those are from Gloria to cheer me up. That dear girl thinks of everything. Buttercups are her favorite flowers because they're so cheery. Don't you agree?"

Hazel nodded, remembering how Gloria had worn a bouquet of them in her cloche hat. The yellow flowers certainly were cheery. "She does seem to take good care of you."

Myrtle sat down and awkwardly picked up the pen. Hazel noticed that her knuckles were swollen. Arthritis. Though Myrtle had very few signs of aging, she'd mentioned she hadn't been spared from that.

"I just don't see how it could've been Wes," Myrtle said. "I mean, I know someone has been doing things around here, but Wes? He was always such a good boy. You don't think it could've been someone at the party, do you?"

"I doubt it. Things were happening even before the party. But Wes was worried if it might be someone from Vera's past."

Myrtle's face clouded over. "We certainly wouldn't have had anyone like that here. Well, unless you count the Rothingtons. It certainly wouldn't have been them. They are very prominent. Old money. One certainly couldn't blame them for not liking Vera, though..."

"You mentioned them before but didn't give specifics. Why didn't they like her?"

"Oh, it all had to do with the crowd she hung about with before she and Wes were married. She's out of that now. Straightened herself up for Wes. But that awful crowd… well, I think I told you before they were no good. Mrs. Rothington's diamond necklace was stolen at a party, right from her bedroom! It was quite valuable, with three large stones in the center and baguettes radiating out from each stone like sunbeams. Well, one thing led to another, and they blamed Vera because she associated with one of those awful boys who were at that party. But that was all cleared up years ago. No one could blame those poor girls for being manipulated like they were by those nasty thugs. The thieves were incarcerated for that job in the end, and all was well."

Hazel remembered Myrtle talking about the bad crowd Gloria had hung about with. Gloria and Vera had been friends even before then, so it made sense that Vera might have hung about with that crowd too. No wonder the Rothingtons didn't like Vera. They probably weren't too keen on Gloria either, which explained the look the girls had exchanged at breakfast the other day when it had been mentioned that the Rothingtons were invited to the party. Of course the Rothingtons wouldn't have killed Vera. That was preposterous. And they certainly wouldn't have been making the attempts on Myrtle because of a robbery that happened years ago. But still, Hazel tucked that tidbit in the back of her mind. It wouldn't do to make assumptions and not follow every lead.

"I just wish this whole nasty business was cleared up." Myrtle sighed and then turned to the letters. The writing looked painful, and Hazel felt a pang of sympathy for her.

"Perhaps a nicer pen would make things easier for you?" Hazel suggested. "I have a lovely Waterman dip pen that Charles gave me. It might make the writing easier, as it has a wide nib."

"Oh, thank you, dear, but I can't use the wide-nib pens, and a dip pen simply won't do. You see the way my fingers are all cramped up? I have to hold the pen like this, and the wide nibs skip across the page, and the dip pens flick dots of ink everywhere. So I'm afraid I'm stuck with using these new, cheaper things." Myrtle shrugged. "But if that's the worst thing I have to complain about at my age, I guess that's not so bad."

"I guess not." Hazel watched her for a few more seconds then said, "May I help you write these?"

Myrtle waved her hand. "Oh, don't be silly, dear. I know you have lots to do. Your time is best used investigating and finding out what your policeman friend is up to. I just wanted to pick your brain and see if you had any inside information on the investigation. I'll be fine here... just close the door on your way out."

Hazel left and headed toward her room. At least one question had been answered. Now she knew why the Rothingtons did not like Vera. Too bad that was a dead end. She'd come in a circle again, just like the detective in her novel. She headed to her room, anxious for Gibson to come back with the information she'd sent him off to acquire. But she'd have to wait on that. In the meantime, if she couldn't make any progress in finding the killer at Lowry House, maybe her fictional detective would have better luck.

CHAPTER TWENTY-FOUR

Hazel retired to her room, her anxiety escalating as she waited for Gibson to come back with his results. The killer was on the loose, and the sooner they were caught, the better. At least Myrtle would be relatively safe. Hazel doubted the killer would try something with the police roaming about the premises.

She opened her notebook, this time picking the Parker pen. She almost had it worked out. The clues which she'd thought had been red herrings had really been actual clues. Even her detective had been fooled by them. But now she needed to figure out how the detective was going to prove his deductions. Would it be by scientific means? Or would he go with a gut feeling? Physical evidence? Shooting holes in alibis? Maybe a deeply hidden secret motive that was only hinted at in the beginning of the book? Either way, she knew she needed to tie the final result together by making sure all the pieces of the puzzle were laid out for the reader to be able to come to the same conclusion as the detective.

"*Meow.*"

"Not now, Dickens, I'm on a roll." Hazel's pen moved quickly across the page, leaving small blobs of ink along with the neatly scrawled words.

"*Meow!*" This time louder.

"In a minute, Dickens." Hazel's detective was about to make a big revelation. Should she choose the dining room or the conservatory?

Thud!

"*Merowww!*"

Smash!

Hazel jerked her attention from the notebook in time to see the small side table next to the bed crashing over. The vase of lilacs smashed on the floor, water going everywhere, flowers lying in a heap of glass. But that wasn't the most astounding thing: Dickens had somehow got into his harness. But in an attempt to wrangle himself into it, he'd got it on backwards. The straps meant to go around his chest were binding his back legs, and he was flailing around like a goldfish out of its bowl.

Hazel leapt up from her chair. "Dickens!" She ran to the cat, stopped him from flopping around, and gently removed the harness. "You pick now to try to use this thing? Did you want to go out for a walk? You have the blasted thing on backwards."

"*Meoooo!*"

Something niggled at Hazel. She frowned down at the harness.

Backwards.

What if the attempts on Myrtle weren't what they seemed? And what if the motive wasn't about inheriting Myrtle's money at all?

Hazel glanced at the vase of lilacs beside her bed then at the lilac notepaper, remembering the note that had brought her here in the first place.

"Oh dear… I may have made a big mistake."

Stuffing Dickens's harness into her trunk so he couldn't get tangled up in it again, she grabbed the letter and ran from the room, hurrying toward the sitting room where she'd left Myrtle.

Myrtle looked up, startled, when Hazel wrenched the door open and bolted into the room.

"Whatever is the matter? Don't tell me someone else has been—"

"No," Hazel said hurriedly. "At least not yet. But tell me, did you send this letter?"

Myrtle frowned down at the lavender notepaper as Hazel placed the letter that had originally summoned her to Lowry House on the desk in front of her. Her face crumbled, and she looked up at Hazel, confusion in her eyes.

"I don't know. I honestly don't remember writing any letter. I know I implied that I did earlier, but my memory has been so bad lately that when you asked about it… well, I just pretended that I *did* write it. It's easier to do that, like with those dishes Edward insisted I buy. I don't want anyone to think I'm losing it."

"But you don't remember writing it, do you?" Hazel persisted. "In fact, that's not even your writing or the same pen."

Myrtle squinted down at it. "I wouldn't use the lavender paper, as that's for the guest room. And it doesn't look exactly like my writing. It's close, but…"

"It's not." Hazel glanced at Myrtle's new pen. She knew the letter had been written with a dip pen that used a wide nib, and Myrtle never used them. "But the question is, do you know whose handwriting it is?"

Myrtle shook her head. "I'm afraid I don't. It looks like an older person's, though, as it's all spidery."

But Hazel didn't need verification. She knew whose writing it was. It was the killer's writing, and she had a pretty good idea of what they were going to do next.

"Where's Wes?" Hazel asked.

Myrtle looked startled at the serious tone in Hazel's voice. "He went to the cottage with Gloria. They were going to—"

But Hazel didn't wait for her to finish. She took off at full speed toward the cottage, fear bubbling up in her chest as she ran into the woods. Would she be in time to stop another murder?

CHAPTER TWENTY-FIVE

Hazel flew through the woods, jumping over roots and dodging squirrels. She should have figured it out sooner. The cameo, Vera's photographs, the buttercups, the Saint John's wort. She'd thought Fran and Edward had lied, but…

She burst into the clearing and raced toward the cottage without thinking. She didn't consider that she was putting herself in danger. Her only thought was to get there before someone else died. And if she were wrong, then no harm done.

Out of breath, she stood in front of the door, wondering whether to knock or just rip it open. If her suspicions were true, then she doubted the killer would open the door for her. She glanced in the window to her right. The house was a mess, photographs and clothing strewn everywhere. Vera's jewelry box lay open on the sofa, jewelry spilling out over the cushions and onto the floor. Wes was seated on a chair at the kitchen table, his head lolling forward. A piece of notepaper was on the table in front of him. Gloria, her back to the door, was bending over the chair. Her right hand was in front of her, and her left was trying to push a blue fountain pen into Wes's hand. It was a Parker dip pen, an older model with a wide nib, Hazel thought somewhere in the back of her brain, even though fountain pens were the last thing on her conscious mind.

Hazel knew what she had to do. She ripped the door open and burst into the room.

Gloria whirled to face her, her right hand slipping behind her back so as to stay hidden from Hazel. The pen slipped from Wes's hand and clattered to the floor. "Hazel. What are you doing here?"

"I should ask you what *you're* doing here." Hazel looked pointedly at Gloria. "Are you hiding something behind your back?"

"What?" Gloria squinted at her as if she had no idea what she was talking about. She brought her hand out from behind her back, revealing a small handgun with a short metal barrel and a bone handle. Hazel knew not to let its small size fool her. It was lethal, especially at this close range. Gloria sighed. "I'm afraid the gun was here the whole time. Wes planned to use it to… to…"

"Schlooook out." Wes glanced up from under his lashes at Hazel, his eyes rolling in his head.

"What's wrong with Wes?" Hazel asked.

"Oh, poor Wes. This has affected him so. I'm afraid he had too much to drink. That's how he deals with stress. Thank God I got here just in time." She held the gun up. "He was going to use this on himself."

"Really? Why would he do that?" Hazel inched her way into the room, a feeling of trepidation coming over her. Unlike the detective in her book, who never made a move without precise reason, Hazel had acted before she'd thought things through, and now she was facing Gloria unarmed. She wasn't sure what she was going to do to get herself out of this now. Somehow she had to get the gun from Gloria.

Gloria glanced at the notepaper then back up at Hazel. "As you can see, he was getting ready to write a note. A suicide note. He said he couldn't take it. He was the one trying to kill Myrtle, but he killed Vera by mistake, and now he can't live with himself."

"He doesn't look like he's in any condition to write a note," Hazel pointed out as she made her way closer to Gloria. Maybe she could distract her with something and grab the gun. Obviously, Wes was going to be no help.

Gloria faltered. "When I got here, he was. He was just getting ready to write it, but I stalled him and was able to get the gun. He must've taken some pills along with the booze, and I stalled him long enough for them to take effect. Now, if you'll just go and get one of the constables, I suppose we'll have to let Wes pay for his crime."

Hazel saw her chance. "Certainly. Why don't you let me take the gun to them? I wouldn't want Wes to overpower you and shoot himself... or you."

Hazel's eyes flicked to a pile of photographs. Photographs! That was what Vera had on Gloria.

Gloria followed her gaze, her eyes turning suspicious as she studied Hazel. Then her mouth set in a tight line. "I was afraid you might be too clever for your own good."

"What do you mean? Just hand over the gun, and I'll get the police—"

"Shut up!" Gloria glanced at the pile of photos again. "I can't take that chance now."

Oops. Hazel should've thought things through more carefully before trying to take the gun.

"I thought you would help me convince the police

that Wes was behind this all along, but you were too clever for me. *Unfortunately*, for you." Gloria glared at Hazel, apparently considering the best way to deal with her. "What gave me away?"

"You made a few mistakes." Hazel knew it was best to keep her talking while she tried to come up with an alternative plan. Too bad she didn't have much experience in that department. In her novels, the detective never needed another plan because he never got himself into tricky situations like this. "For one, you used the lavender notepaper to summon me to Lowry House. It's the same paper in my room."

Gloria blanched. "I was hoping you wouldn't notice that. That *was* a mistake. I didn't want to send the note on the Rose paper that I use, and Auntie would have wondered why I wanted a sheet of hers, so I grabbed from one from one of the rooms. I had no idea Mrs. Naughton would put you in there. But what tipped you off that it was *me* who used the notepaper?"

"When Myrtle asked, you claimed that you were never in that room."

"Naturally. I didn't want to be linked to the lavender paper."

"Right. That was smart. That's what I would have one of my characters do, except you made one little mistake. Apparently, when you were in the room getting the paper, a sprig of buttercups must've fallen off your hat. Dickens found them later on, underneath the chair. So, you see, when you said you weren't in the room, I became suspicious."

"That's it?" Gloria screwed her face up. "Those flowers could've come in from the hallway. That would never hold up in court."

"That wasn't the only mistake you made." Hazel kept one eye on Gloria while also trying to look around the room for a weapon. "You lied about being at Gull Landing to provide yourself an alibi for when Myrtle's pills were switched." Hazel bluffed—sort of. She felt pretty confident that Gibson's inquiries would prove that Gloria hadn't been at Gull Landing. Even though he hadn't confirmed her suspicions yet, the startled look in Gloria's eyes told her she'd been right.

"That doesn't prove I switched her pills. You still have nothing on me. And neither do the police. Which is why they're going to believe that Wes is the killer, and when you confronted him, he had to kill you, too. I tried to wrestle the gun from him, and Wes was shot in the struggle. I was lucky to get out of here alive." Gloria gestured for Hazel to get in front of Wes's chair, and Hazel slowly shuffled in that direction. Gloria bent down as if to place the gun in Wes's hand so as to point it at Hazel, to make it look like he shot her from the chair.

"I don't think they're going to believe that once they realize your true motive." Hazel sidled closer to the sofa. Why hadn't she told Myrtle to send the police? She would never let the detective in her novels confront the killer alone without a weapon, and now she'd gone and done it herself.

"Don't be silly. I don't have a motive to kill Auntie. I won't inherit a thing from her." Gloria struggled to get Wes's limp hand around the gun.

"Not Myrtle. You never intended to harm Myrtle. But you wanted it to *look* that way. That's why you summoned me here. Because you knew I would look into it and find all the clues you'd cleverly placed for me."

Gloria hesitated. "So you worked it out. Too bad for you."

"I always thought the attempts on Myrtle seemed a little halfhearted. How clever of you to be there when she fell on the path, to make sure she didn't get hurt, and to prove that you couldn't possibly be the one trying to harm her. And I'm certain you made sure that only a few of her pills were switched so it wasn't a lethal dose. Oh, and did you use the Saint John's wort to make it seem like someone was poisoning her, or did you want her to be confused so she wouldn't catch on to the fact that you were the one behind these attempts?"

Gloria barked out an unpleasant laugh. "A good attempt. But no one will believe that. Not that you'll get a chance to tell them. It sounds like fiction. Like something a novelist would come up with. I doubt the police would agree with you."

"But they do," Hazel said. "Detective Chief Inspector Gibson noticed right away there was something suspicious about the attempts on Myrtle. He checked with Gull Landing and the antique jeweler just this morning. So you see, it would be best if you just handed over the gun."

Gloria's eyes narrowed.

Hazel reached out for the gun, but Gloria only aimed it at her with more determination. "You're bluffing." Gloria gestured with the gun more harshly now, and Hazel scooted over a few inches, backing up closer to the sofa. From her position, she could see out the window. Was someone coming through the woods? If only she could stall Gloria for a few more minutes.

"The police will be here any minute, and your sentence will be much worse with three murders instead of one."

Gloria snickered. "I'm not falling for that old line. Is that something that happens in your novels? You think you're so smart. But look where it's got you. Shot by Wes before he turned the gun on himself."

Hazel glanced out the window again. Hope flickered in her chest. Someone *was* coming through the woods! Gibson. He must have already checked Gull Landing and the estate jeweler and come to the same conclusions Hazel had.

Click.

Hazel's eyes jerked back to the gun. Gloria's thumb was on the trigger.

"It won't do you any good. The police know all about you," Hazel ventured.

Gloria frowned. The gun wavered. "They do not, and besides, there is no proof."

"Of course there is. It's right there." Hazel gestured to a pile of photographs, and Gloria's eyes jerked to the photos, her brows slashing into a frown. Hazel took the opportunity of Gloria's momentary distraction to step closer to the couch, groping along behind her for the heavy jewelry box she'd seen lying there. "You didn't find the photograph, did you? The one Vera was blackmailing you with? That was why you set this all up, wasn't it? So that you could kill Vera and make it *look* like she was mistaken for

Myrtle. With all the fake attempts and having me to help convince the police, you thought they wouldn't look too closely into Vera's death."

"I looked all through these, and there *is* no photograph. I searched the house from top to bottom when Vera and Wes went to the doctor. And with no photograph, I have no motive, so the police would never accept your story. But Wes had motive to want Auntie dead, and he had means and opportunity, too. Wes has rat poison and the spade in his shed. I should know because I put them both there when I was weeding the garden for him. Wes missed with the arrow because of his hand and then threw the bow down in the path. Wes killed Vera. And now Wes is going to kill you."

Hazel saw Gibson burst into the clearing just as Gloria's finger twitched on the trigger. Hazel only had a split second to react. She grabbed the jewelry box and hurled it toward Gloria.

CHAPTER TWENTY-SIX

The jewelry box hit Gloria square in the forehead, and she stumbled back just as she fired the revolver. The bullet shot past the side of Hazel's head then slammed into the ceiling just as Gibson burst through the door.

"Hazel, are you all right?" Gibson's face was dark with concern for Hazel as he rushed to disarm Gloria.

Hazel patted her coif and answered him calmly. "I'm fine." But her attention wasn't on Gibson—it was on the jewelry box. It had smashed to the floor and broken open, revealing a secret compartment on the bottom from which a photograph was hanging out.

"What is going on?" Gibson had taken the gun and was wrestling a protesting Gloria into handcuffs.

"I checked the places in your note. Your suspicions were on the money. I realized the intended victim never was Myrtle but couldn't work out who the killer was until I checked Gull Landing and the jeweler's. Then I realized it was Gloria all along… but why?"

Hazel picked up the picture. "I should've worked it out earlier. Some things just didn't add up. As you said, the attempts on Myrtle all seemed too easy."

Gibson slid his eyes toward Wes, who was slumped in the chair still. "And Wes never had anything to do with it."

"No, it was all Gloria. She killed Vera. But you were right, it wasn't because she mistook her for Myrtle; it was because Vera was blackmailing her with this." Hazel turned the picture to face Gibson. It was a picture of Gloria in a lavish bedroom, holding up a diamond necklace of three large stones in the center and baguettes radiating out from each stone like sunbeams.

"That's not true!" Gloria wriggled and struggled under Gibson's grasp. "It was Wes all along. So what if Vera has a picture of me."

"It's not just a picture of you, Gloria. It's a picture of you with Mrs. Rothington's stolen necklace. The one that your friends went to prison for." Hazel turned the picture back to look at it. "And if I'm not mistaken, this picture was taken in Mrs. Rothington's bedroom while you were stealing it."

Gloria struggled even harder. "I was coerced! It was Vera who wanted to steal it!"

"Nice try. Even if it was her, you were an accomplice," Gibson said. "Too bad, because now instead of a small prison sentence for stealing Mrs. Rothington's necklace, you're going down for murder."

"The Rothington necklace? Is that what this was all about? I thought they caught those thieves." Constable Lowell appeared in the doorway, and Gibson gestured for him to take custody of Gloria, who was still struggling and trying to come up with excuses.

"Apparently, not all of them. We can thank Hazel for finding the last one." Gibson turned admiring eyes toward Hazel, and her cheeks flamed. "Just how did you work that out, Hazel?"

"It was nothing, really. I mean, I'm sure you would've come to the same conclusion if you'd been privy to the same information I was. You see, I knew that Gloria and Vera had been friends before and had run with a bad crowd. Before the party, someone had mentioned that the Rothingtons didn't like Vera. After her death, Myrtle confided the reason—Vera used to hang around with some of the boys who were arrested for stealing the necklace. But I didn't put two and two together until my conversation with you, Chief Inspector Detective Gibson." Hazel nodded at Gibson, and she noticed a sparkle in his eye.

"Oh? And what conversation was that?"

"The one about assumptions. I realized I *had* been making assumptions. I had assumed because Gloria knew about the attempts and had been helping to ensure no one else hurt Myrtle, that she could be ruled out as a suspect. I never checked her alibi for the day of the pill mix-up. And I also assumed that Vera would've been the one to sell the cameo, when I should've easily realized it was Gloria because Gloria lied about being in town that day. I did try to check that lie, but when I went into town, I made another assumption. I saw an employment agency and assumed Gloria was looking for a job and didn't want anyone to know. Myrtle had told me she didn't have much money."

Gibson nodded. "But that's not why she was there. The jewelry store assistant told me that *Gloria* was the one who sold him the cameo."

"I realize that now. Vera's cameo is right here." Hazel picked up the cameo from the pile of jewelry. "Gloria had to sell hers to get the blackmail money for Vera. That's how Vera was buying all her expensive jewelry."

"Gloriashhh cha Skiller," Wes mumbled, his head lolling.

Hazel was startled. She'd almost forgotten about Wes. He was drugged and needed help. She rushed to his side. "We know that, Wes. Everything is alright now." She squatted down and peered up at his face. He was pale, his eyelids fluttering as if he were struggling to stay awake. "We should get the doctor for him."

"I'll send for one right away." Constable Lowell rushed off with Gloria, who was still trying to talk her way out of it.

Gibson turned stern eyes on Hazel. "Hazel, I don't want you to think your help isn't appreciated. It would have taken us a long time to realize what was really going on without your information. Sharing information is good, but honestly, you should have let the police confront the killer. It's dangerous."

Hazel lowered her eyes. "I realize that. But when I saw Myrtle writing letters in the sitting room and I realized that it was Gloria who had written the letter that brought me to Lowry House in the first place, it all clicked into place, and I knew that she was trying to implicate Wes. Myrtle said they had come to the cottage, and I was afraid of what she might do to him. I ran off without thinking."

Gibson's face softened. "Well, everything turned out all right in the end. But there's one thing that I don't understand. How did you know the photograph would be found in the jewelry box?"

"Actually, I didn't. But I knew Vera would've had to have had some sort of physical evidence to blackmail Gloria with. Then I remembered the photographs. Vera was an amateur photographer. And Wes had told me that Gloria was keen on organizing the photographs. But from my observations, Gloria and Vera were not great friends anymore, so why would she want to help her out?" Hazel said. "I didn't realize it would be *in* the jewelry box until the very last minute, though. When I had inspected the jewelry box before, I had noticed it seemed rather shallow on the inside for the size of the box but never considered it might have a secret compartment where Vera had hidden the photograph. Though I'd like to say I knew the box would smash and reveal the picture, in all honesty, I was actually just using the jewelry box as a weapon. She was pointing the gun right at me, and I didn't want to get shot."

Gibson laughed. "Seems like you picked the right item to throw. And I'm glad you weren't hurt *this time*.

But next time, please leave the task of confronting the killer to the characters in your novel."

———————

THE NEXT DAY…

"I CAN'T BELIEVE that whole business about someone trying to kill me was a farce." Myrtle frowned at Hazel over a cup of tea. They were seated in the front sitting room with Fran, Edward, and Gibson as Hazel waited for Duffy to pick her up. She'd sent word through Giles after Gloria had been arrested. Now that the mysterious goings-on at Lowry House had been put to an end, Hazel was anxious to get back home.

Wes was in a room upstairs. Dr. Fletcher had pronounced he would be perfectly fine, though Gloria had apparently mixed sleeping pills in with his whiskey. According to Wes, she'd brought him to the cottage so he could get some of his things and suggested they have a drink. He started to feel groggy shortly after, and he only vaguely remembered Hazel and the police bursting in.

"Apparently, you were in no danger," Hazel said.

"In fact, Gloria really did want to keep you safe. It was Vera she was after."

"I can't say I didn't see that coming"—Fran nibbled on a scone and glanced at Myrtle—"the two of them never did get along. I always knew there was something funny going on there. I mean, I didn't think Gloria would *murder* Vera, though."

"What alerted you?" Edward asked Hazel. Upon Gloria's arrest, he'd cancelled his trip to London to stay and make sure Myrtle wasn't too upset in finding out her favorite grandniece was a killer.

Hazel laughed. "Believe it or not, initially, it was Dickens! He tried to put his harness on backwards, and that's when I realized we had the whole case *backwards*. We thought someone had killed Vera because they had mistaken her for Myrtle with the red hair and the bejeweled gloves, but it was really Vera who was the target all along, and the attempts on Myrtle were only laid out to throw us off course. Gloria set those attempts up to make it *look* like someone was trying to harm Myrtle. That's why the attempts were not dire enough to actually kill her. I should have paid more attention to my gut instincts on that account. I always thought the attempts seemed a little half-hearted to result in murder."

"Well, Gloria had us convinced!" Myrtle said.

"Yes, but I should have known better, especially after I saw Gloria and Vera arguing outside my window." Hazel frowned and glanced down at the red-and-black hound's-tooth cat carrier where Dickens was ensconced at her feet. "Funny thing— overhearing that conversation was also due to Dickens. He wanted the window open, and when I opened it, I overheard them outside."

"*Mew.*"

Hazel continued, "I didn't hear what they said, but it sounded as if they were fighting, and then Gloria got in the car and took off. Later on, she said she never left the house that day. And I'd felt the undercurrent of the little barbs that Vera would shoot at Gloria. But I never suspected Vera was *blackmailing* her."

"Or that Gloria was using me to set it all up." Myrtle sounded sad.

"Unfortunately, she did. She had Vera's murder planned from the start," Hazel said. "Wasn't Gloria the one who suggested you henna your hair?"

Myrtle patted her hair. "Yes. She said it would keep me looking younger."

"And it does, Gram," Fran said.

"Yes, it does," Hazel agreed. "But it also served another purpose, because Vera used that same henna.

And when your jeweled gloves were itching on the night of the party, I bet it was Gloria who suggested you remove them."

"Why, yes. She even offered to take them so I didn't have to be bothered with them. You know, she bought me those in the first place..." Myrtle frowned. "Oh. She might've been planning it even back then."

"I'm afraid so. And when she took them at the party, she probably brought them straight to Vera, knowing how much Vera loved sparkly things."

"But how did she get Vera to go into the library?" Edward asked.

"I don't know if she necessarily needed her to be in the library or just away from the party. Somewhere dimly lit where she could have her back to the door and it would appear that she was mistaken for Myrtle, with the red hair and the gloves. Early on in the party, I saw the two of you"—Hazel nodded toward Fran and Myrtle—"sharing a drink with Vera and Gloria. I thought it was nice that everyone was happy and drinking together, but now I wonder if Gloria hadn't taken that opportunity to slip something into Vera's glass."

Fran gasped. "Why, I thought it was odd that Gloria came over and suggested we have a birthday toast for Myrtle. How could we refuse? You mean she did that on purpose to drug Vera?"

"Yes. She must have slipped something into the glass ahead of time. I remember Wes saying that Vera was acting as if she were drunk but that she hadn't even had that much to drink. Now we know why."

"So all these attempts on Mother were contrived by Gloria so that she could eventually kill Vera?" Edward seemed incredulous.

Come to think of it, it *was* a crafty plot. Hazel almost wished the villains in her books were as clever and meticulous as Gloria had been.

"Yes," Gibson said. "It didn't take her long to confess the whole thing to Constable Lowell last night. She verified that she made sure she was with Myrtle the morning she would fall on the pathway so she could keep her from getting hurt. She lied about being on holiday at Gull Landing so as to provide an alibi, when in fact she sneaked into the house and switched the medicines. She'd been feeding Myrtle Saint John's wort in the health elixirs, just enough to upset her stomach and cause minor confusion. She knew how sharp Myrtle was and decided keeping her in a state of confusion would help prevent her from getting suspicious. And she snagged the revolver out of the wardrobe at the cottage when Wes and Vera went to the doctor in London. She'd searched for the photo, too. Was quite indignant that it was all Vera's fault, because if she hadn't hidden the photo so well, Gloria would never have had to shoot her!"

"She sounds a bit unstable," Edward said.

Gibson nodded solemnly. "She may try to claim insanity, but I don't know if it will stick. She planned things out too thoroughly. She confessed that, on the night of the murder, she steered Wes toward the library. She had the gun hidden in the dumbwaiter in the hall, as the staff never uses it anymore. Once they had Vera seated in the library, she acted as if she were agitated about not being able to find Myrtle, and Wes ran off to help. Gloria simply sneaked back and shot Vera through the back of the chair. With this confession, there's no denying it was premeditated. And, of course, with all the other things she's done to make it look like Myrtle was in danger…"

"Now that I'm thinking about it, *she* was the one who brought up all these little incidents. I never even suspected anything until she started talking about them," Myrtle said.

"All a part of her plan," Hazel said. "She wanted you in her confidence so that you wouldn't suspect her. Even more so when I came, so that you would already be able to show that you were confiding in

Gloria and we would think she couldn't possibly be the killer."

"I dare say, it was quite clever of her to send for you, Hazel," Edward said.

"Indeed." Gibson looked at Hazel with admiration. "But in the end it turned out to be her downfall. I don't know if we could have solved the case so quickly without Hazel."

Hazel blushed and waved her hand dismissively. "I hate to admit I was taken in it first. She fed me the clues the way she wanted me to see them. I should've been more observant that morning when the arrow was shot. Gloria was the only one who knew we were sitting in the arbor. She had been with us, walking the path, and we'd told her we would be going to sit there. Since she was an excellent shot, she shot the arrow so as to narrowly miss Myrtle. Then, knowing I would give chase, she threw the bow on the path that led to the stone cottage and disappeared off into the woods."

Fran frowned. "You mean that day I happened across you and Gram with the arrow sticking out of the arbor really wasn't because it was an errant shot? I wondered about that, but you both said it was an accident. I never thought someone was trying to shoot Gram."

"Well, since we didn't know about the other attempts, I don't see why you would have." Edward slid his eyes from Myrtle to Hazel. "Which makes me wonder. Why didn't you tell us about the other attempts? Were we suspects, too?"

Hazel shot a look at Gibson, hoping that he would run interference for her. She didn't want Fran or Edward to feel bad or be mad at Myrtle. He caught her look and nodded.

"Of course. In order to do a thorough investigation, Hazel knows that everyone in the house would have to be a suspect. Vera and Wes as well. And Edward, you and ? had the most motive to want Myrtle dead," Gibson said.

Edward blanched. "Me? Well, I hardly would kill my own mother."

Myrtle reached over and patted his arm. "Of course not, dear, but we had to be cautious. We couldn't leave any stone unturned."

Fran made a face. "What about me? Why would you suspect me?"

"You weren't one of our main suspects," Myrtle assured her. "But you do have that strange affinity for the Pembroke cameos, and it does make you seem a little off."

Fran's hand flew to the brooch at her throat. "I

saw that brooch at the estate jeweler and assumed Vera was selling it. I went in and demanded to know where they had got it. I got a bit hotheaded and am embarrassed to say I made quite a scene." She slid a glance over to Hazel. "That's why I told you not to dally in town that day. I was afraid you would go to the jeweler's and find out about it. I thought it was Vera because she never appreciated the cameos, and she had all that new glittery stuff. I guess Hazel wasn't the only one who assumed incorrectly."

"Now, now, dear." Myrtle clucked. "Don't feel too bad. It's not a bad thing that you love the family cameos. In fact, we have a little surprise for you." Myrtle nodded toward Edward, who pulled a black velvet box out of his pocket and passed it to her.

"I had your father go to town and collect this early this morning. We can't have the family cameos being sold in an antique jewelry shop." She flipped the lid to reveal the cameo Hazel had seen at the antique jewelers. Then she pushed the box over toward Fran. "This is for you, dear. I want you to have it."

Fran's eyes went wide as they flicked from the cameo to her grandmother. She took it out of the box lovingly, and then for the first time, Hazel saw a real, true smile radiate across her face. "Thank you, Grandma."

Myrtle smiled at her fondly. "You're welcome, dear. I'm just so upset about Gloria. She'd finally sorted herself out, and now this." Myrtle shook her head. "But now I'll have to focus my efforts on taking care of Wes. I'm feeling much better now that I haven't been drinking those health elixirs. My stomach has been fine, and I haven't been confused at all." Myrtle frowned. "And to think my dear grand-niece was doing that to me. Anyway, Wes needs our help now. He's quite broken up, and it's going to take him a while to get over this, but we can't let him sink into depression."

Fran put her arm around Myrtle. "Don't worry, Grandma. I'll take care of you better than Gloria did. Since Gloria was always hovering around you, I never got a chance to care for you myself."

"And I'll help out with Wes," Edward said. "He needs a man to bond with. I can take him to the club and keep him busy. Don't worry, we'll sort him out in no time."

"Wonderful." Myrtle beamed at Fran and Edward. "I'll have Mrs. Naughton make sure there is always a room for the two of you here, in case you want to stay for extended periods."

Hazel saw Duffy pull up outside, and her lips curled into a smile at the thought of her staff, who would be tripping over themselves to hear about the case. She was sure Duffy would pepper her with questions the entire ride back to Hastings Manor. Outside, Giles rushed to the car with Hazel's suitcase.

"Well, I'd best be going." She stood and picked up Dickens's carrier and turned to Myrtle. "I'm sorry about Gloria but glad you weren't harmed."

Myrtle stood and hugged her. "Thank you, dear. So nice of you to come to my rescue. I do appreciate it." She bent over and peered into Dickens's carrier. "And you, too, Dickens."

Edward and Fran both rose and shook Hazel's hand. "Thank you for your help."

Gibson stood, grabbing the handle of Dickens's carrier. "I'll help you with this."

Hazel relinquished the handle, though she had half a mind tell him she could manage on her own. She bit her lip. It wouldn't do to be making an enemy of Gibson. He might come in handy on other investigations, and she had to admit she kind of liked having him around.

As they exited out the front door, Gibson's mouth curled into a smile. "I know your staff is anxious to hear about your trip."

Hazel shot him a glance. "What do you mean?"

Gibson shrugged. "They've been very eager to find out what was going on at Lowry House."

"How do you know that? Have you talked to my staff?"

"Mrs. Dupree brought me some of her famous biscuits." Gibson stowed Dickens's carrier in the backseat of the car then opened the passenger door for her.

Hazel raised a brow. "I didn't know she brought you biscuits." Though, now that she thought about it, she wasn't surprised. She knew Alice had been trying to get the two of them together, and what better way than to ply him with her delicious biscuits? Well, it wouldn't work. Hazel was not the type to be set up. And she wasn't in the market for a new husband. Though, if she was, maybe she would consider Gibson.

But she couldn't bother herself about Alice's biscuits. She had important work waiting at home. She'd finished the last part of her plot the night before. Turned out, she really could write a book on her own.

Gibson shut the passenger door and stood at the open window. "I do appreciate your help with this case, but I hope I won't find you in the middle of my next investigation."

"*Mew.*" Dickens made his opinion known from the backseat.

Gibson glanced into the backseat to address Dickens. "You either."

Hazel laughed, and winked at Gibson before signaling Duffy to move forward. "I wouldn't dream of getting into the middle of your next investigation, Detective Chief Inspector Gibson. Wouldn't dream of it."

****

Will Hazel and Dickens investigate another case? Find out in the next book in the Hazel Martin Mystery series:

Murder by Misunderstanding (Hazel Martin Mysteries Book 2)

SIGN UP for my email list to get all my latest release at the lowest possible price, plus as a benefit for signing up today, I will send you a copy of a new Leighann

Dobbs book that hasn't been published anywhere...yet!

http://www.leighanndobbs.com/newsletter

IF YOU ARE ON FACEBOOK, please join my VIP readers group and get exclusive content plus updates on all my books. It's a fun group where you can feel at home, ask questions and talk about your favorite reads:

https://www.facebook.com/groups/ldobbsreaders/

IF YOU WANT to receive a text message on your cell phone when I have a new release, text COZYMYS-TERY to 88202 (sorry, this only works for US cell phones!)

Cozy Mysteries

~

Regency Matchmaker Mysteries

***

An Invitation to Murder (Book 1)

Hazel Martin Historical Mystery Series

***

Murder at Lowry House (book 1)

Murder by Misunderstanding (book 2)

Mooseamuck Island Cozy Mystery Series

* * *

A Zen For Murder

A Crabby Killer

A Treacherous Treasure

Lexy Baker Cozy Mystery Series

* * *

Lexy Baker Cozy Mystery Series Boxed Set Vol 1 (Books 1-4)

Or buy the books separately:

Killer Cupcakes

Dying For Danish

Murder, Money and Marzipan

3 Bodies and a Biscotti

Brownies, Bodies & Bad Guys

Bake, Battle & Roll

Wedded Blintz

Scones, Skulls & Scams

Ice Cream Murder

Mummified Meringues

Brutal Brulee (Novella)

No Scone Unturned

Blackmoore Sisters

Cozy Mystery Series

* * *

Dead Wrong

Dead & Buried

Dead Tide

Buried Secrets

Deadly Intentions

A Grave Mistake

Spell Found

Mystic Notch

Cat Cozy Mystery Series

* * *

Ghostly Paws

A Spirited Tail

A Mew To A Kill

Paws and Effect

Probable Paws

Silver Hollow

Paranormal Cozy Mystery Series

***

A Spell of Trouble (Book 1)

Spell Disaster (Book 2)

Magical Romance with a Touch of Mystery

***

Something Magical

Curiously Enchanted

Contemporary Romance

***

Reluctant Romance

***

Regency Romance

* * *

Scandals and Spies Series:

Kissing The Enemy

Deceiving the Duke

Tempting the Rival

Charming the Spy

Pursuing the Traitor

Captivating the Captain

Romantic Comedy

***

Corporate Chaos Series

In Over Her Head (book 1)

Can't Stand the Heat (book 2)

What Goes Around Comes Around (book 3)

Sweet Romance (Written As Annie Dobbs)

Firefly Inn Series

***

Another Chance (Book 1)

Another Wish (Book 2)

ABOUT THE AUTHOR

USA Today bestselling author, Leighann Dobbs, discovered her passion for writing after a twenty year career as a software engineer. She lives in New Hampshire with her husband Bruce, their trusty Chihuahua mix Mojo and beautiful rescue cat, Kitty. When she's not reading, gardening, making jewelry or selling antiques, she likes to write cozy mystery and historical romance books.

Her book "Dead Wrong" won the "Best Mystery Romance" award at the 2014 Indie Romance Convention.

Her book "Ghostly Paws" was the 2015 Chanticleer Mystery & Mayhem First Place category winner in the Animal Mystery category.

Find out about her latest books and how to get discounts on them by signing up at:

http://www.leighanndobbs.com/newsletter
Connect with Leighann on Facebook
http://facebook.com/leighanndobbsbooks

This is a work of fiction.

None of it is real. All names, places, and events are products of the author's imagination. Any resemblance to real names, places, or events are purely coincidental, and should not be construed as being real.

MURDER AT LOWRY HOUSE

Copyright © 2017

Leighann Dobbs

http://www.leighanndobbs.com

All Rights Reserved.

❋ Created with Vellum